Thursday's Child

Thursday's Child

SONYA HARTNETT

CANDLEWICK PRESS
CAMBRIDGE, MASSACHUSETTS

First published by Penguin Books Australia, 2000

Copyright © 2000 by Sonya Hartnett

First U.S. edition 2002

Library of Congress Cataloging-in-Publication Data

Hartnett, Sonya.
Thursday's child / Sonya Hartnett. —1st Candlewick Press ed.
p.   cm.
Summary: A young woman, looking back on her
childhood, recounts her family's poverty, her
father's cowardice, and her younger brother's obsession
for digging tunnels and living underground.
ISBN 0-7636-1620-6
[1. Poverty—Fiction. 2. Family life—Fiction.
3. Farm life—Fiction.] I. Title.
PZ7.H2285 Th 2002
[Fic]—dc21   2001025223

2 4 6 8 10 9 7 5 3 1

Printed in the United States of America

This book was typeset in MJoanna.

Candlewick Press
2067 Massachusetts Avenue
Cambridge, Massachusetts 02140

visit us at www.candlewick.com

For Henry M. Saxby

Now I would like to tell you about my brother, Tin. James Augustin Barnabas Flute, he was, born on a Thursday and so fated to his wanderings, but we called him Tin for short. He wasn't my youngest brother, because it's right to count in Caffy, but I never saw Tin an old man or even a young one, so he stays just a boy in my mind. Tin's bound up in childhood forever, as far as my recollection goes, although the last time I saw him he was wizened and looking ancient as the hills. Memory is eccentric, how it stalls when it wants to. The dogs that we owned—I don't remember a single one of them ever being a puppy. They were born antiquated and rickety, those hounds, whelped under the veranda with their prime well and truly past them. Da when he was in his moods would sometimes threaten to shoot the lot of them, but

Mam would put a stop to that. Mam had a heart too soft for herself—her heart got put in the wrong body. Her heart wanted to do its living somewhere clement and florally. Her face would crush as if that misplaced pump of hers was agonized and she would say, "Don't you touch a hair of their heads, Court Flute. God loves old dogs."

"Now Thora," he'd say, contrite and holding his hands in the air, "you know I never meant to."

So the dogs got away with being dozy and good for nothing and never bailed up so much as a possum with the excuse being their venerable age, and Tin got away with being young, though wizened, and something of a curiosity in the surroundings, and never had to answer for being grown-up and sensible. God loves old dogs and children and kept things, at our house, the way He wanted them.

It's proper I mention Caffy because Caffy was born the day Tin learned to dig and everyone says that if it hadn't been for Caffy coming then things might have been different, though no one really believes that's so. Everyone knows Tin was born to burrow, he was born to the task like a hare or one of those white blind hairless moles that comes into the world itching to get its claws into the safety of the ground. And what that means is that, if Caffy hadn't come, if I hadn't taken Tin to the creek, if it hadn't been such wet weather or we'd lived some other place, things would have started an alternative way, but started nonetheless.

Mam had been groany most of the time Caffy was getting up to be a fully fledged baby, and on the day he was finished and ready Mam was groaniest of all, and the mood in the house was dire. My brother Devon took off for help with having the delivering done, my sister Audrey was locked away attending Mam, and Da looked worriedly down at little Tin and me. He scooped Tin to him and gave him a kiss. Tin wasn't mad for being caressed, he was never as fond of anyone as everyone was fond of him and you could see poor Da would have liked to hold him forever, as though Tin were comfort or a shield. But Tin turned his cheek, and with a sigh Da freed him. "Harper," he said, "take your brother and go to play."

I didn't dispute, just did what I was told. I was glad to get away. Tin, he was too young to know what was going on. He was only four at this time. He came uncomplaining, although at that age he didn't usually like to go far from the shanty and would fret and whimper if its roof went out of sight. He came that day, however, quiet as a mouse.

I took his hand, which was a clenched flower bud. I felt a touch sorry for him because it might be his last day of being the baby of the family and his coddling days could be done. He was too small and knowledgeless to know it, though, so I guessed the loss couldn't hurt him. Besides, his being born was what put an end to the coddling days of my own. "Come on, Tin," I said, and gave his arm a bit of a yank, for vengeance.

I didn't know where to take him or how long Da wanted us to stay away and I was worrying, too, about Mam, who'd been gasping and muttering back at the house. When we reached the crest of a lumpy hill I turned to look behind me and saw the shanty with the dogs lying in the gray sunlight and Devon's summer bed folded on the veranda and no grass, just earth and slime, in a wide circle all around the building, and beyond the circle the grass began and you could see where Tin and I had stomped through it, patches of it being trampled. Our house had two windows and one of them looked into the bedroom where Mam had been pacing all morning, but I had no hankering for going and peeping through. It felt like something dangerous was going on in that room. I knew a fair amount about babies, being almost seven years old at this time. I knew that delivering meant coming into the world, not arriving on the doorstep like a package. And I'd experienced my share of newborns; there'd been one arrive between me and Tin, which I had seen and didn't remember, and one between Tin and this latest, which I hadn't seen and did. The first lasted only a moment and the other not even that, so I reckoned babies coming shouldn't cause all that much trouble. They either came and stayed, or came and didn't. Only a baby, but everything seemed dismaying somehow, everyone was so grim. I didn't want to be anywhere near the place.

The land where we lived was by nature dry and dusty but that winter there'd been more rain than a duck would have dreamed of and when I glanced at Tin the mud was seeping up between his toes and he was sinking into the earth, shivering and half asleep. I shook him wakeful and hurried him along. "Where will we go, Tin?" I asked, not expecting any answer because he was generally reticent. "Will we go fishing?"

I had him moving at a trot and his head was joggling up and down, which I took to signify his agreement. There weren't any fish in the creek but he was at the age where you can fool them. He was certain to start whining sooner or later, anyway, no matter what we did, and the best I could do was stall that commotion as long as I could. I had a pin in the hem of my dress and I stopped to unfasten it and give it to him. He examined it carefully before looking at me quizzically through tangles of dandelion hair. "You can spike a fish with that," I explained. "That's your hook."

I could see he liked that sharp reflecting thing. It was half a mile to the creek and I put him on my back and hiked him most of the way, he being light as a feather. I talked to keep him distracted, telling him it was callous to stab my throat with the pin and what would the baby be, a new boy or a new girl? We had two of each already, not counting Mam and Da, so things were pretty equal as they stood and it would be a hard blow to the side that came away the minority. I thought it was a shame that only babies could be born, whichever it turned out being. I could think of plenty of other things I would have preferred to get for nothing.

The creek was typically a drool of a waterway but that afternoon it was running high because of all the rain and the bank was soft and oozy; Tin's feet disappeared to his ankles and he was covered in mud before he even reached the water. He was a dark child anyway, so it didn't look too bad on him. I set on a rock and left him to his devices and looked around, bored. There were white-trunked trees on either side of the creek and you could see where the rain had washed away the earth that had hidden their roots and the roots poked out knotted and naked, groping. It was that quiet, cold kind of day when the birds are surly and refusing to sing and the leaves on the branches aren't moving and seem like they never could. The creek was sluggish, hardly rippling, made from something thick and heavier than water. I was hungry, and could hear my stomach rumbling. I would have exchanged a new baby a hundred times over for a plate of something warm to eat.

When I looked again at Tin he was crouched staring and musing in the shallows with the seat of his pants drenched black, so I crawled forward to see what was diverting him. There was a fish there, swimming in his shadow. There was a whole crowd of fishes, when I looked harder, stranded in a pocket of rock as if the creek had splashed them there for safekeeping or for Tin's amusement alone. "Oh!" I exclaimed. The fish were the length of Tin's thumb, each of them, and not worth the hooking, but they were pretty and silvery, they looked like that hem pin come alive. Tin was sucking on the pin so I took it from him and stirred the rockpool's water and the fish spangled and flashed in agitation. I put a finger in the water and the whole crowd darted and tapped and knocked and nibbled. Tin's teeth were clickering with the cold now; he crossed the steppingstones to the opposite bank and from the way he tugged despondently at a handful of tree root and looked mournfully in the direction of home I could tell he was pondering the practicality of crying. He wandered a distance upstream, clutching the bank to steady himself, hoisting his knees so silt and water came pouring off his heels. "Tin," I said, "come and look at the dainty fishes."

He wouldn't; he turned his face to the mucky wall of the creek and stood there, up to his knees in water. I wasn't about to pander to his childishness so I took no notice of him. I caught a fish in the bowl of my palm and it lashed about while the water drained between my fingers and then lay flat on its side, heaving like a bellows. I petted it with a fingertip and touched it to my lips. It didn't taste like anything. "Look, Tin," I said, but he went on masquerading to be deaf. So, "Look, Tin," I said again, this time making my voice full of wonder and amazement which he could surely not resist, same as a cat can't resist investigating when you suggest there's something hidden she might like to see. If it works on a cat it should work on a four-year-old, but it didn't. Tin stayed where he was and when I glanced over my shoulder full of annoyance, he wasn't anywhere. And the creek bank looked different somehow, with clots of dryish earth rolling down its flank and plinking into the water and the ground all about torn through with a great cleave, and I could hear the dog-scratch sound of tree roots tearing. The creek bank had caved in, right on top of Tin. There was not a spot of him left to be seen. That tiny fish I had in my hand went slithering into the water.

I pounced through the creek to where he'd last been standing and started scrabbling at the dirt, yelling out his name. The earth was heavy and sticky; my fingers left slick gouges behind them but hardly took anything away. I screeched to him over and over, thinking if he could hear me he'd be comforted, all the while thrashing at the mud, spattering it into my hair and eyes and spitting it out with my cries. I dug and dug in a frenzy, my arms moving like legs running, but I couldn't get a decent grip; I was staggering and slippering and weighted down with the cold, I was gasping and choking and the earth slid into the places I'd dug clear and spat clammily into my face and blinded me from what I was doing but not doing, changing but leaving the same. I tripped in the water and it went over my head, dashing the muck from my eyes but alarming me anyway because the water shouldn't be that deep, and as soon as I was on my feet I realized why it was that way. The creek was damming around the landslid earth in its midst; it wasn't getting past the way it wanted to and each minute was raising it higher. In rage I splashed the water and kicked it, as if a beating could drive it away. There was a full-grown stringybark looming on what was left of the bank and it let out an ominous crack like lightning can and I wailed at it and pleaded to it, knowing what it intended to do. My arms were going and my voice was going but everything in me was off and running; the water was rising and the tree was falling and dirt was tumbling more and more into the places I'd just that moment cleared. I saw this water and how heavy the mud was and how useless and slow were my efforts and I knew that Tin wasn't alive under there, he'd been drowned or flattened by the weight of that terrible sludge, so I turned and fled after the rest of myself for home. I ran like a bird flying. And while I ran, shrieking inside as I was and hollering for Da aloud, there was a voice clear as a bell in my head that said I was glad to be running, and getting away. If I found help, it wasn't going to be only me who couldn't get him out.

The door of the house was open and Devon was standing alongside the threshold but I charged straight past him, making for my Da who sat slouched with his head down, and I was sprawled across his lap before he even knew I was there. He hauled me up by the armpits and shook me out like a sheet. I remember how wide and round his eyes went as I babbled out the thing, how the mud from me jumped onto him, how when he dropped me I was already sprinting for the door.

And then the three of us were bolting through the paddocks, Da overtaking me and Devon just as though the bullet in his foot had never even happened though we'd all seen the scar, never asking me where we were going but heading right for the exact spot as if Tin were reeling him in. Some of the more sprightly dogs were loping along beside us but soon gave up through exhaustion.

Da he splashed through the creek and threw himself against the dark face of the mudslide and set to work like a madman, using his arms to tear away sloughs of earth that slopped into the creek and smeared the water green. The stringybark was moaning and splitting, holding its place for dear life. Da looked at it once or twice without stopping digging. Devon and I were digging too but it was Da doing most of the work: he hacked away at the mud in a fury, kicking great hunks of it aside, and when he stumbled in the slickness he didn't pause but ripped off handfuls of the stuff as he clawed his way upright. Devon and I were screaming but Da was saying nothing, his teeth jammed into his lip; after a time he started hissing and I made out he was hissing words. He was saying, "Take the new one instead. Take the new one instead."

And the water was rising so Da was standing with it to his knees and Devon to his thighs and I to my waist, the three of us twice our thickness with the freezing mire that we couldn't make any less of and the tree was creaking pitifully, its leaves weaving a shuddering waltz, and it is the horriblest loneliest, saddest memory I own. I wanted to say we didn't need to hurry, there was nothing to hurry for anymore since Tin had been entombed for easy half an hour, but I knew Da would clout me if I said a thing like that. I stepped away because I didn't want to be the first to touch him, to catch a lock of hair in my fingers or scratch his soft cheek with my nails. Da and Devon didn't notice me. Da's fingers were clubs and he stooped to wash them and make them useful again and that's what I remember best—that Da's hands were clean and white when it happened. He hadn't touched those hands to the mud when another hand, a small and grubby flower bud, a tiny little lost doll of a hand, broke through the earth and landed flat in Da's glistening palm.

Da had him out in a second and there was Tin, shiny with slime with his curls plastered to his head and his clothes clamped close as a second skin, dripping dirty water and blinking at the light. He was juddering with coldness but he wasn't crying; he gazed at us through eyes as blue as sky, them and the whites of them being the only bits left colored as they should be. Da hugged him to his heart and burst out weeping—noisy weeping, that shocked me—I never saw my Da, before or afterward, do anything like that, and Devon and I were riveted to the spot. Weeping and clutching Tin, he turned for home, plowing through the water and up the opposite bank. Devon and I lingered where we were, panting from the effort and twitchy with the shock of it all. I reached a quaking hand into the depths of the mudslide and put a cautious eye to its wall; why hadn't Tin been drowned or flattened, is what I wanted to know. By rights he should have been. And you could see clearly why. That old tree had saved him. A chunk of earth had been sucked away from its roots and had left behind a cave that closed Tin up and kept him snug and safe as a nesting bird, if slightly damp and tickled.

"Have to chop it down now," said Devon, considering the tree.

Marks from Tin's fingers were preserved in the gunge: "Look!" I said, impressed by the sight. "He did more digging than we did—he dug his own way out!"

"He's only a kid, Harper. How's he going to dig himself out?"

Devon was scornful, so I didn't bother explaining. We had hardly made a dent on our side of the mud, I knew; if any useful digging had been done, it had been done by Tin alone. Devon wouldn't believe it, so I kept the knowledge to myself. We splashed through the water and ran to catch up with Da. He was off in the distance and I could see Tin's small face with his chin on Da's shoulder, staring back steadily at where he had been. I knew I wasn't wrong, and Tin knew what he'd done, all right.

When I looked into Caffy's frightful newborn face I thought, You're the one Da would have exchanged for Tin. He would have put you in the mud instead. Not because Da had anything against Caffy but because Caffy had no meaning yet and because he had a good chance of dying shortly, anyway, based on those that had gone before. It must be terrible, I thought, to be such a nothing that you could be bargained away. Tin was Da's pet, of course, but it relieved me knowing he hadn't offered to exchange Devon or Audrey or myself, either. We weren't pets, but we weren't nothing. Caffy was nothing. Da didn't so much as glance at the baby until he'd got Tin washed and dressed and bundled in a quilt before the fire.

Mam was apparently battered but we were allowed in to see her by Mrs. Murphy, who'd done the delivering, and Devon blurted out the story of the mudslide to her, giving himself a heroitude in the telling which he had not had in reality. Mam made Da fetch Tin and settle him beside her and if the baby thrived that would be the last time he'd be allowed to lie there, I suspected, though he'd slept all his life close to her heart. Thing about babies is, they take over everything, being louder than they are capable. Audrey grabbed me by the ear when Mam was distracted and dragged me wincing into the other room. She gave me a lash of abusing and finished off by snarling, "How could you let Tin get caught in a mudslide when you knew Mam was having a baby?" and flipping me over the head with the flat of her hand. I wagged my tongue at her when she was back beyond the curtain and went and hunched in front of the fire to lick my wounds. Mrs. Murphy was sitting there, goo-cooing at the baby. "You've got to be careful, Harper," she said to me. "You're grown-up now and responsible."

I didn't say anything, only seethed and rubbed my stinging pinched ear. If I could answer for mudslides, I would have made one slop over Audrey before another minute went by. She had a haughty streak of righteousness in her, she was as bad as someone religious. Mrs. Murphy tried to console me by waving the baby under my nose and when I saw his skewwhiff head and face like a louse peering out from under an ash heap, I couldn't restrain from opining that I'd never seen such a hideous and peculiar-looking coot in all my life, and got cast into the paddocks with a whack from Mrs. Murphy's free hand. I went and sat cursing on the mullock heap where I'd stopped with Tin, before the day had turned sour on me. I could see the house the same as I'd seen it earlier and I was in no hurry to get back to it, just like before. The shanty didn't look any different but now there was someone else living in it and it occurred to me, Where are we going to put him? While he was inside Mam's stomach Caffy hadn't taken up much more space than if it'd been Mam on her own, but now he was born he would need a cradle, or at least a box or drawer. The house only had the two rooms and it was cramped already. Da would laugh and ask, "What do you expect for nothing?" And Mam would say, "It wasn't for nothing, Court." When I was young I never understood what she was talking about, because Da was right about the nothing.

Our shanty had been built by a prospector, who hadn't needed space indoors; it was dirt that interested him, and there was plenty of that. All over the paddocks were mounds of the stuff that he had dug out and piled up and grass was growing on them now, they'd turned into land. Da had barriered the snaky old shaft but Devon and I knew how to get into it and we'd scratch at its walls in the darkness, searching for the dusky glimmer of gold. We never found anything and neither had the miner, he'd died empty-handed with only the echoing shaft and the slab-hut shanty to show for his efforts, and Da said the government boys would never have given us the land if there had been anything beneath it worth keeping for themselves. But Devon had great faith in that miner as having been unlucky rather than deluded and he used to pan the creek some days, and his fingers would freeze frigid blue. He was saving to buy a pony and because three years of doing so had rewarded him with only a scatter-ing of black shillings, finding gold became the quicker way for him to get where he was going. He had never ridden a pony and we didn't have a fence to pen one in but he had his plans and a name picked out already: Champion. Devon and that pony: you never saw anyone so demented.

If there was gold no one could see it, but there were trees with lacy leaves and the creek which dried up completely most summers and off over the horizon was ground that was all ours, tawny red ground the color of a fox's coat sprouting tussocks of grass that were not green but rather silver, which rustled like paper in the breeze and burned like tinder if you put a spark to them, and we had neighbors who had things the same. Most of the neighbors weren't farmers and neither were our Mam and Da but the others were somehow more fortunate than us, more blessed than us our Mam said, and coaxed crops and vegetables to grow. We never could, and Da said our land must be particularly exhausted or maybe simply sullen, a bad patch maybe poisoned, so we trapped rabbits instead. There were plenty of rabbits around; the earth was bouncy with them. Da and Devon went trapping most days and Da would sit on the veranda for hours on warm evenings wiring snares as delicate as cobwebs and near invisible to the eye. Snaring was time-consuming but gave a pelt without a hole and missing the hole gave a pelt an advantage when there were rabbit hides galore for sale. We had racks standing beside the house and there were always a few flyblown skins pegged baking in the sun and the dogs knew better than to have a go at them. Once a month Da would hitch a lift on the rabbito's cart and take his pelts into town and Devon would wash the racks while they were empty, the suds falling pink on the ground. The flesh from those flayed rabbits was stewed up by Mam and in bed at night I could feel it, stringy between my teeth.

I was almost seven and accepted life as it came: I lived on exhausted land that was given to us by the government boys because of what my Da had done for his country during the war; in the war my Da got a bullet in the foot and the scar was gnarled like a tree stump; my Da shot rabbits now and my Mam made rabbit stew. My name was Harper Flute, and I was small for my age but I would grow; I had a gap where a tooth was still coming down and I could bend my thumbs backward until they touched my arm. I had chores to do each evening and five days of the week I went to school, where the Devil himself would get into me and my knuckles would be striped for his trouble. I had an older sister named Audrey and my brothers were Devon and Tin; there'd been a baby born today, and he was to be called Caffy.

I saw Da come out of the house and trudge along the path that led to where I was sitting and I tensed because I thought I might be in for another whacking, making it my third for the day, and sure enough he said to me, "Did you call that baby ugly?"

"No, Da, I never did."

"Harper. Are you telling lies again?"

"No, Da!"

He squinted at me. "That baby," he said. "He's got a pointy head."

I bit my lip and gazed at him.

"He's not near as bad as you were, though, the day that you were born. You were the scaringest thing I ever clapped eyes on. Face like a dropped pie."

"Da!" I wriggled with delight.

"It's true, I tell you. Your Mam will have to pray about this new one same as she prayed about you. 'Please, Lord,' she'll say, 'have mercy, don't make us live with this gruesome sight forever . . .' You'll see he'll improve, chicken, when he gets over the surprise of being born. You getting a wet arse down there?"

"It's not too bad if the grass is under you."

He nodded; he sat beside me and we were side by side with our elbows on our knees. I said, "I didn't mean to let Tin get caught in the mudslide. I told him not to go near the water, I told him it wasn't safe. It was just an accident, Da. Audrey twisted my ear."

"Hurt?"

I nodded somberly. Da wiped hair from his eyes.

"She was wrong to do that to your ear. No one can do anything about mud. It's one of those things that has a will of its own."

I knew he was remembering being a soldier: Da said that in the war a whole country had changed into mud. The muddy country had suctioned down entire bodies of men and horses and no one saw a hair of them again. Da said that the soldiers would dig and dig frantically, spurred on by gargling screams, but the mud had a teasing nature and would suck its captive deeper just as the shovels were finding him, just as hands were reaching to clasp. The last thing the diggers would see might be a glimpse of face, a howling mouth suddenly silent or an eye rolling plaintively to them, the fight and disbelief gone at the end, quelled by grief and fear. A man in the mud was a condemned man, Da said, and arguing with his fate would only break your heart for you. I wondered if Da had thought about that country when he'd heard what had happened to Tin. He must have, I reckoned—I reckoned he was in this mood, this sunny joking carefree mood, because he believed he had argued with Fate for the right to Tin, and had won. He liked it, thinking he had done the rescuing himself, so I didn't say anything about Tin scratching his own way free.

Da was right about Caffy: by the time a handful of months had passed the shape of his skull shifted until his head was as round as a ball of clay and just as soft to touch and he filled out his skin the way a child grows into a bigger brother's clothing, the wrinkles all smoothing away. He looked like a newborn angel, with Da's fair hair same as Audrey and Devon, with Mam's blue gaze same as Tin and me, with lashes like fawn butterflies wafting over his eyes. He had a drawer of the dresser for a cradle but mostly he slept curled like a pup in the crook of Mam's shoulder, his pink-lipped mouth making a circle around his dream. He was placid and cheery throughout the day but I fancied he was afraid of the dark: when he woke at night he would sob not with need or outrage but with a plaintive drag of misery, as one who has just heard the most harrowing news. This sad, sad weeping would wake all of us and I'd move nearer the warm light of the fireplace; Devon would pull his pillow over his head and, beside me, Audrey would heave a martyr's sigh. Tin wouldn't make a sound but I would see the glint of his eyes blinking in the glow coming off the embers. Da had built a small pallet for him and set it up at the foot of the bed I shared with Audrey, and sometimes when Tin was sleeping there his hands would flutter, seeking the old close comfort of his Mam. He used to sometimes study the baby, not touching or smiling or doing anything you could put a word to. He would watch Mam walking about the kitchen with Caffy gumming on her collarbone and he'd have that same vigilant, studious expression on him. It made Mrs. Murphy decide he was nothing less than a seething mess of murderous jealousy and he should never be left alone with the baby. "Tin's just looking," said I for him. "He isn't doing any harm."

That was back chat, and her eyes slid up and down. "Remind me of your age, missy."

"I'm seven now."

"Seven, is it. I wish I were seven again. Life's a simple thing, at seven. Ignorance, as they say, is bliss. Outside with you, my girl, where you ought to be."

And then, one day, Caffy became ill. He started off in fine fettle but by evening he was arching his spine and loosing banshee shrieks of pain, slumping with exhaustion at the peak of each screech and heaving in air to screech anew. Mrs. Murphy was summoned and gazed with delight upon him: sick infants were her reason for being, she thought there was nothing nicer and more pleasingly dreadful. She knit her brows and clamped her teeth and commanded us to stand aside. She pressed her hands to Caffy's stomach and Caffy squealed blastingly. His face was scarlet as a plum and his fingers were clawed like a demon's. "It's colic," said Mrs. Murphy. "A blind man could see it. I will have to stay."

The weeks that followed were a morbid and mysterious time, full of whispering and tiptoeing and Mrs. Murphy's celtic prayers. She had her bags brought over and claimed Da's side of the bed and bedroom, where she would always be close to the child; Da was banished into Devon's bed and Devon was shunted to the veranda, though the nights could still be cool. Colic might last a week or a month or a fortnight or you could be laying out a body within a day or two, and there was no way of foretelling which way a baby would choose to go. "I've seen them bonny in the sunrise," said Mrs. Murphy, "and cold as a whistle by noon." She told

Devon and me to stay outside except in emergency, and to welcome every opportunity for being useful. Older brothers and sisters, she suggested, had saved the lives of infants in the past simply by being useful. I was ready and willing to make a heroine of myself and imagined the admiring tales that would be told of me, but my enthusiasm waned when I discovered that being useful meant carting buckets of water up from the creek so the baby could be soaked in them. I was only slight, not brawny, and the buckets were awkward and heavy to lug through the fields; Caffy would flail with his fever and every drop that splashed on the floor would give me a knifelike pang. Nothing anyone did seemed to make Caffy get any better so, in a poignant piece of usefulness, Devon and I found a picturesque site for his grave. His dying would be unfortunate because we'd become fond of him in the months we'd had him but at least Mrs. Murphy would go home then, and we wouldn't have to carry water or hear his squallering anymore.

It was the wailing that was blamed, at first, for Tin carving out his hideaway beneath the shanty's veranda. "What's that child doing down there?" asked Mrs. Murphy, her head cocking like a sparrow's.

"I think it's quieter," said Audrey. She was sitting on the veranda's edge where she came regularly to sigh.

"He could go into the paddocks if he wanted quiet," I pointed out. "Anyway, he can hear the baby through the floor, probably. That's not why he's there."

"Why, then, Harper, if you're so clever?"

We could see the bright shine of Tin's eyes peeking out at us. He'd crept under the veranda three days earlier and scooped from the earth a shallow which contained him agreeably. If you reached under the veranda you could touch the tip of his nose. If you put an eye to a chink in the boards and squinted, and if the light was falling right and the moment was a lucky one, you could make out the silk of his hair. "He just likes it, that's all."

"But what is he *doing*? He must be *doing* something."

"He's doing nothing. He just lies there and watches."

"Watches what? And why's he watching it?"

"For no reason, he's watching nothing. He comes up for bedtime and his tea."

Mrs. Murphy looked withering. "Well, at least he's keeping out of the way."

No one but me took any notice of Tin during the next few days, because Caffy was at his worst— Devon scouted for a gravestone. Da took the slug gun and a crib of johnnycake and went out for rabbits each morning, his face white and haunting. Audrey stayed inside with Mam and Mrs. Murphy and the three of them hovered above Caffy's drawer as though frowning at him might frighten the illness away. After school and between fetching water I passed the time with my hands pressed against the walls of the house, talking through the shadows to Tin. Sometimes he would stop his work and listen; sometimes the job of improving and extending his lodgings was of vital concern and puffs of dirt would fling out while I spoke to him, and go drifting down my throat.

"You liked it, didn't you, Tin? Yep, you liked it, that dark. Da came running and so did Devon, and I was running, too, we were thinking you'd been killed under all that muck and by rights you should have been but you weren't, you weren't even frightened. You liked it, you thought it was fine. You didn't want to come out but you knew you were breaking your poor Da's heart, so you took pity and started digging. And you liked the digging, didn't you, even better than you liked the dark.

You liked the feel of that dirt on your paws . . . Tin?"

Sometimes he'd listen; sometimes I'd hear the scraping of his nails.

"Tin. You're only small, you're only a boy and not much use for anything, but I know something about you. You like the dark and you can dig. You can do it good and well. Audrey shouted at me when the mudslide squashed you, but I didn't mind. She's always shouting, so it made no difference to me . . . What are you doing, Tin? Where are you going?"

I'd be very still when I spoke to him, like you must be still around a bird if you want a look at it. You couldn't see him, now, if you crouched at the edge of the veranda—he'd gone much farther beneath the house. The shanty was built on a slope and the stumps under the veranda were tall, tall enough to let a chicken pass with just a ruffling of feathers on her crown; at the rear of the house the stumps were much shrunken and a cat needed to crawl to get by. Tin was digging round abouts in the pitch-black center now, grubbing out a bowl of earth that was deep enough to stop him bumping his head on the underside of the floor but shallow enough to keep him warm and secure. At sunrise he would begin his excavations, the sight of his bare feet slipping away the last you would see of him until twilight.

And then, one evening and suddenly, Caffy was better. The redness soothed away from him as if someone had pulled a plug. Da had swapped his cigarettes for a bottle of medicinal brandy and there was enough left of it for him and Mam and Mrs. Murphy to fill the three best glasses, and we children were given water flavored by an orange. We sat on the veranda and the sunset stained Caffy's cheeks pink as he dozed in Audrey's lap, a thinner infant now, with that scrubbed and bewildered expression that a fever leaves behind. Talk, which had been for so long about the baby, finally found its way on to Tin.

"He's been down there a fortnight," said Mrs. Murphy. "It isn't natural and I won't let anyone say it is. A child needs fresh air and the sun on his head."

Mam was putting plaits in my hair and I swiveled my eyes to Mrs. Murphy. She knew a good deal about children, especially considering she had none of her own.

"He'll come out now the distress is over, Rose."

"You want to be sure he does, Thora, and soon."

"I think that, while he's content down there, we should let him be."

I rolled my gaze to Da. He gave me a sharp wink and a sly grin. Mrs. Murphy was tisking.

"Leaving him be is the last thing he wants, Court. The boy's beggaring for attention."

"Then giving it to him will just be encouragement."

Mrs. Murphy gave a cross little bark. "He's not taken well to the arrival of the tot. You saw how he was, sulky, and suspicious."

"Tin's not jealous of Caffy," I told her, same as I had told her before.

"Then why won't he come out?"

"Because he *likes* being under the house." Gawd, she was dense. "He likes digging—"

"Harper." Mam twitched my hair.

"I know jealousy when I see it." Mrs. Murphy set her jaw. "I'll be proved right, time will tell."

Audrey was waving a hand above Caffy's pearly face, whisking away the flies. "What does he do all day?" she asked. "Only dig?"

Mam was finished and I scuttled from her reach, two skinny plaits sprouting like weeds behind my ears and already unraveling from their bows. "He's not really digging—he's not digging tunnels. He's just changing the shape of things."

"He eats his dinner under there," said Devon, licking the taste from his glass. "It's disgusting."

"He's only been doing that for a few days. He used to poke out his head and arms."

Mam asked, "Will he come out if I call him, Harper?"

"Maybe."

"Tin!"

"You needn't shout. He can hear."

"Tin? Tin, would you like to chew the orange rind?"

We waited, Da and me bent over the veranda railing so we'd be the first to see anything, all of us deadly silent in an effort to hear something, but all we heard was the trees blowing in the quiet, and Tin did not appear. "There you are," said Mrs. Murphy. "Green."

"You call him, Harper," said Da. "He might come for you."

I knew he wouldn't, and hesitated. "He's not a dog," I muttered. "He has to have a reason."

Da smiled. "Well, let him be. He'll think of his bed when the night gets cool and we'll see him then."

I bit my nails and must have looked shifty. "Harper?" asked Mam.

I slouched and sighed, pushing my kneecaps around. I said, "When he thought everyone was asleep last night, he snuck out and went down there again."

"And stayed out all night?"

"Mmm."

"Without a blanket?"

"Nnn."

"I knew I heard a noise," said Devon. "I thought it was rats."

"Now, Thora, he'll catch a chill—"

"The dogs care for him," I cut in quickly. "The dogs go under there and sometimes they help him dig. They would have curled up with him and kept him warm."

Mam was looking dazed by all this; she was staring ahead at nothing. "Harper," she murmured, "is he filthy?"

"Oh no, he's only dirty."

"A splash of dirt never hurt a fella." Da vaulted the railing and knelt in the grass, craning to see under the house.

"That depends on the dirt, surely," said Mrs. Murphy. "How is he attending to the needs of his bladder and bowels, is what I would like to know."

"Like a cat," I told her. "He digs, and he buries. He's dirty, but he's clean."

Devon grinned and Da hawed, and even Mam and Audrey and Mrs. Murphy smiled. It made me leap about and yelp excitedly, "He's *clever*, Tin is *clever*, he's only five years old and he's doing this all by himself!"

"Clever he may be, but no good will come of it. Stop that prancing, child! It's absurd for him to be hacking away beneath the house. Absurd, Thora! He'll be mashed like a snail if the house drops on him."

"Pass me the light, Devon." Da held the lamp under the boards and I saw its yellow beams glowing through the cracks. "I can't see him. I see a dog, but I don't see him."

"You never see him unless he wants you to."

"Court," said Mam, "is the house stable, do you think? I don't want him hurting himself."

"The house will be standing when Tin's an old man."

But Mam had been spooked. "He never wanted to hide before the young one was born, did he? I don't think he did."

Da straightened and poured himself the dregs of

the brandy and thoughtfully drank it while we leaned forward and waited, holding onto our breath. He said, "Tin is not the jealous kind, Thora. It's not the baby who's to blame. Tin just likes being under the floor, I reckon. There's something about the place that pleases him. He'll grow out of it, and making a fuss in the meantime won't hasten things. He's not harming anyone or anything, being where he is."

I was delighted, for I had been making a daily diversion of Tin's dusty escapades, but I was tinged with some spiteful greenery, too — I knew that, had it been me beneath the shanty, Da would have drummed me out smartly and then tanned my hide.

"It's your decision," said Mrs. Murphy, clapping her thick hands on her knees. "All I'll say is, I'm glad he's yours and not mine. I've worries enough without mothering a boy who thinks he's half rabbit. I'd put a blanket out for him, Thora, if you're going to let him have his head. Dogs have fleas, and he'll be drained bloodless before long."

It was a good thing in the end, Mrs. Murphy weaseling into Mam's head the idea that Tin must be jealous of the baby. Mrs. Murphy had intended the qualm should curb Tin somehow, but it didn't work that way. Rather, keeping Caffy safe and close meant setting Tin free, to do as he pleased. Caffy stopped Mam from stopping Tin even when she saw how far he had gone from us, how distant he was leaving her behind. And when a day came that proved Caffy's coming and Tin's going had nothing to do with jealousy but were coincidence and nothing more, it was much too late for Mam, or for me or for Da or for anyone, to change his ways, even if we wanted to.

Time passes slowly when you're young, and quickens as you get old. Summer lasted forever when I was seven, but now it only visits. When I was seven the days had more hours than I had use for and the distance between sun up and down again was a vast and lazy sprawl; now, when I look back, things seem to have happened with the most hectic and startling speed. The weeks and months have seeped into each other and become a span without feature and detail, riddled with cavernous holes. I remember Caffy with the pink on his cheeks the evening we talked about Tin under the house, but I don't remember him learning to crawl. In my ragged-edged memory he is, one moment, a babe in Mam's arms; the next, he is walking and talking. I don't remember the weeks that followed that evening on the veranda but I remember when I stopped thinking it was strange, to have a brother living beneath the floor. I remember this because I remember seeing Tin standing in the yard with his shadow stretching away from his feet, and thinking, What is he doing there?

In summer when the heat was such that you could see it like a ghost or a genie, wavering and writhing without being visible at all, someone was always under the floor with him, hunkered down in the special place he'd gouged and kept brushed smooth for his guests. If Mam or Da was huddled there, there wasn't room enough left for anyone else, but Devon and I could squeeze in together and Audrey would sometimes bring Caffy, who would fidget and be bored. I liked it best when I was alone there, with space to stretch and put my chin to the cool ground. We used to tell him what was going on above his head although I knew he could hear everything, anyway, and most of what we said was stale news to him: Da would say, "There was a red-back in the firewood, you should have heard your Mammy shout," and Devon would say, "I got another deener, Tin, I found it on the road." Mam had fits of worry and would try to drive him out occasionally, threatening him with snakes seeking shelter and tempting him with a corner of the big bed, if sleeping in the big bed was what would mollify. She said he would listen but not hear her, that he was deaf to her wishing. I decided that he heard too much, not being particularly interested, anyway, so I used to lie and be silent with him, watching him work and musing on matters of my own. Sometimes I would fall asleep and I never slept so peacefully as I did those summer afternoons, cooled by the earth that was always in shadow, walled off from the sun and the wind, waking to crickets tuning their violins and to the restful searching sound of Tin's plowing hands. He crafted the dirt so carefully, piling it this way and that, shoring it up and feathering it away. Underground amongst it you could see how he worked in a halo of light that filtered between the shanty stumps and lit up his skin, which was whitening already, and his eyes, which would consider you brightly before turning to work and away.

One day he was most occupied and didn't pause to sit and stare at me awhile, as was his typical way, so I squirmed as far under the house as my head would let me and spied on what was involving him. He was crouched in the center of his territory, the place where darkness gathered at its thickest and the halo from outside never shone. I said nothing until my sight sharpened to make out what he was doing and then I gave a squeak of thrill. I had been waiting to see what I finally saw, expecting it every day—it was the logical step for Tin to take. I backed out and ran to tell everyone that Tin had started work on a tunnel. At last he was expanding his empire, having taught his hands the language of the dirt, to understand its quavers and tremorings, to trust its sturdy promises and to read its crumbly mind. Everyone came to contemplate what he'd done but I was the only one small enough to wriggle far enough and see it with my own eyes. The tunnel wasn't deep yet, being hardly more than a hole, but its walls were precisely circular and you could tell it was solemn and serious. The earth from its innards was scattered about but there wasn't much of it, hardly more than a powdering; later we would notice that Tin left almost no evidence of his industry behind him and for years I could not understand how that was done. Da was asking what I could see and I shouted a description of the tunnel and when I glanced awkwardly over my shoulder I could see my family on their bellies, captivated and staring.

"Bring a bowl of water," Da told Audrey, and when it came he slid it beneath the house as far as his arms would go. "If the walls of your tunnel are damped down and dried out, Tin," he said, "they might hold together good and strong."

"Court," Mam murmured, "maybe we shouldn't encourage him . . ."

But Da was back with his eyes at the gap, not listening, straining to see. Tin was considering the water. After some thought he dipped a hand in it and dabbed his wet fingers to the mouth of the tunnel. "He's using it!" I shouted, and heard Mam tisk crossly and Da laugh triumphantly. Every day, after that, he made sure there was a bucket of water set down by the veranda. Some days Tin used it and we'd find the empty pail rocking where it had been flung; other days he ignored it for the dogs to lap away. He knew what was best, he knew when and what was needed. Overnight the tunnel became deep enough for him to stand in, and within a week it doglegged sufficiently to hide him away.

One day Da came to me and he was holding the arched head of a pickax, its peeling hide crackling and rusted black and blue. He said, "Look at this, chicken. I found it by the mineshaft. Buried to the hilt it was, but the dirt washed off pretty well. It must be fifty years old, this—see how the handle's decayed?"

I could see, all right, and I felt the weight of it when he put it in my arms. "Go and give it to Tin," he ordered, and I did as I was told. Tin climbed out of the tunnel and received the pick head warily, for it was as long as his legs and as heavy as himself. He did not touch it while I was looking, and regarded it from the corner of his eye, but Da seemed content. "He'll mull it over and decide whether he has a use for it or not."

I trailed him through the paddocks where he was doing the rounds of the closest rabbit snares and after a time he said to me, "What are you thinking, Harper?"

"Nothing, Da."

"Yes you are. You're sucking your fingers in your thinking way."

I pulled my fingers from my mouth and tucked my hands behind me. Da frowned from under the brim of his hat. "You've been in mischief, have you?"

"No, Da, I swear!"

His blue eyes kept me prisoner a moment before letting me go; there was a rabbit at his feet and he bent a knee to work at it. This rabbit was a dead one, because sometimes they died of fright. If they weren't dead already, Da would break their necks by whacking them over his thigh. But this one was as stiff as bark, its body stretched as long as it would go. Da shook it loose of the snare and flipped it back and forth, to check that it was sound.

I blurted, "You like Tin being under the floor, don't you, Da?"

He glanced at me. "Why? You thinking about going down there yourself?"

I grinned, squinting against the lash of my hair. It was a hot dry day and blowy and the leaves on the trees were thrashing together furiously. "No, Da! It's just—Mam doesn't like it, is all I mean."

"She doesn't mind too much."

"But she gets mad sometimes, when she talks about him."

Da carried the rabbit over his shoulder, where it stuck out like a horn, and I scurried in his streaky shadow as we walked on to the next. The grass had died and left bald, red, crack-riddled earth behind it; ants were pouring from the cracks and charging around everywhere, racing over my bare toes. "I reckon that's just natural mother-feeling," he said. "Children can be taxing."

"But you don't mind about Tin. You gave him the pick, to help him."

He said nothing and it might have been that he

hadn't heard, what with the wind frothing up the leaves and the stones gritting under his boots. So I said more loudly, "You don't mind Tin digging. I thought it would remind you, maybe."

"Remind me of what?"

"Of the mud."

Mam always said we weren't to talk to Da about things like the mud, but she'd never told me why. Now Da stopped walking with a sudden jolt that made me leap backward, wildly regretting my words. But he simply looked at me, his hands gripping rabbit legs. He said, "The mud in the war, you mean?"

I nodded cautiously. "You said it used to break your heart."

"It did do that."

He used the rabbit to swat an insect and went on, and I followed him quietly. He started talking, waving a hand to ward off flying bugs.

"In the war, the one thing I wanted to do to the very best of my ability was dig. An important man, a general, once told the boys, *Dig, dig, dig, until you are safe.* We spent most of our time trying to do as that general said: we lived in trenches that we dug and dug over because they were always falling in and filling up with water and getting blasted sky-high. I was forever digging, but I never could do it the way I wanted. I could point a rifle and jump a wire and I was handy at doing those things, I knew I could do them well, but I could swing a shovel and do it all day if I had to and never be pleased with my work. I could never dig deep enough or careful enough or quick as I wanted. I could never dig until I was safe, as that general had told me to do."

I stared up at him, and he down at me. We had come to the next snare and there was a live rabbit caught by the toes and it was leaping up and being yanked down, landing with a thump and a gritty plume. "Tin could have done it, though," Da said. "Tin could have dug for the whole battalion. Tin's got a talent. He has a gift."

"Is Tin digging to get safe?"

"I reckon he must be."

"But why? There's no war now. What does he need to be safe from?"

Da looked at the rabbit, which was pitching itself in circles in a cloud of dirt and fur. "Maybe you don't need to be safe from something, Harper. Maybe you can just be *safe*—I don't know. I only know that, in the war, I couldn't dig to save myself, and I wasn't safe because of it. Maybe Tin is digging because every skerrick in him is demanding that he do it, and that's what will keep him safe. He's doing just as that general told us to do, as if he heard it for himself. So I won't hinder him, if digging is what he wants, and I won't let anyone else hinder him, either."

By the time Tin had been under the floor for a year everyone for miles around had heard about his subterranean dwelling, and in the early days some of those at school had to be menaced for making mockery and only afterward learned to respect it, but most were admiring from the start. All of them came visiting, at one time or another, to have a squiz for themselves, but there was little to see. The adult neighbors couldn't squeeze beneath the house far enough to inspect the tunnel, and the children they sent under could only come out agreeing that what we said was true—there was a tunnel, all right, but it arched away so steep and swarthily that they couldn't see Tin or anything. Da made a law that none should go into the tunnel because that was Tin's domain, and everyone thought this an excellent rule. It was not an inviting prospect, descending into that blackness. When the schoolteacher came yammering about Tin being or not being educated, Da bent the rule a curve. He said that, if the teacher could catch him, he was at liberty to fill Tin's skull with whatever learning he cared. The teacher glanced beneath the house and shiveringly confessed to being queasy of small spaces, and went away alone.

Gerty Campbell, whose property faced ours from the opposite side of the road and who had a turned eye to which I devoted hours of gruesome contemplation, pinched her lizard lips at the very thought of Tin. She spoke in fierce clipped sentences, as if her time was ticking down. "Should have warmed his backside at the start. Thora dear. Hear me. When will you put an end to this nonsense?"

Mam only smiled and looked at the ground. That was what she did, by the time a year had passed, when anyone asked her about Tin.

"Thora dear. Did you hear? Should have warmed his backside. Time he came out."

"I've asked him to come out, Gert, more times than I can count. And sometimes he does, to please me. But he's a bird in a cage, up here. I don't want him here as a prisoner."

Gerty said, "What rubbish."

Jock Murphy, who was married to Mrs. Murphy, had this to say another day: "That's a wild child you've got there, Court. It's gone a year and he won't come up of his own accord now, I'd say. You're letting him have his head, then? You're going to let him do as he pleases?"

"That's right, Jock. I think that's best."

"And Thora?"

"Thora knows what I think."

Mr. Murphy whistled. "Plenty of others would have tied him to the veranda post to keep him above the ground."

"You tie dogs and mules to posts," said Da.

When Mr. Vandery Cable came snooping, he suggested we fetch buckets. "Pour water down the tunnel," he said, "and soon enough he'll bob up like a cork."

All of us were gazing at Cable's elevated shanks—the rest of him was down in the dirt, his eyes leveled under the house. All of us were hardly breathing. Vandery Cable was a high-and-mighty man about the district, the richest person that anybody knew, and him calling on anyone was understood to be a most honoring thing. He made his money out of pigs.

"Tin hasn't learned to swim," said Mam. "He'd drown, if we did that."

Cable stood, slapping his knees. "Not much difference in him being drowned or otherwise, far as I can see. It's lucky you've got these spares, Flute, because that one's not much use to you. He certainly isn't earning his keep."

Da smiled lamely around the nail he was chewing. Cable looked at Devon. "You know what they do on a farm to an animal that isn't earning its keep, Devon?"

". . . Get rid of it."

Cable nodded. "Get rid of it. That being the case I'd say it's fortunate you couldn't call this place a farm, isn't it?"

Devon glowered but Cable didn't note it, he was considering the yard. He asked, "What you got growing, Flute?"

"Nothing yet, Mr. Cable."

"Nothing. How many years have you been here? Ten?"

"Round about eight, I'd reckon."

"Eight years. What have you been doing with yourself, besides breeding? This whole place should be cropped."

"Our land's exhausted," I informed him, and Cable's eyes swiveled to me. He was a tiny man, hardly bigger than Devon, with a head of thick black hair and dainty little feet at the end of his scanty body, and his eyes rolled smooth as marbles at the bottom of a pail. He wore wing collars even with his work clothes, and nothing he wore ever dared to crease, whenever you saw him he was all mockered up, as neat as a beetle in its shell. "Be a waste of time trying," I added.

"Would it now, missy?" He eyed me a disquieting moment, and I hid casually behind Audrey. He looked, then, at Caffy, who was slapping drooly hands in the dirt. "I don't envy you, Flute," he said. "I wouldn't like to have my fortune hopping around on the ribs of some rabbit. Skinning isn't going to keep these squibs fed when they're older, with appetites to match. You want to put your mind to earning, and do it now. You got a piece of land here, so make it work for you."

"You're right, Mr. Cable, but, you see, I've never been a farmer—"

"That's easy to say, Flute, and I don't doubt you'll say it until you drop dead from starvation." He strode across the yard to his jinker, haranguing over his shoulder. "You've got responsibilities and it's time you took hold of them. You aren't a farmer. Fine: become one. Farming's no more difficult to learn than anything else. You've got your laborers already born to you. You could put that little digger to use plowing. He'd be cheaper to feed than a horse, anyway."

He climbed onto the jinker and yanked the reins of his own horse rudely, making it clop about. "Tell you what," he said, peering down his nose. "I'll take Devon off your hands and have him taught to string a fence. That will be a start. Accumulate experience from those that have it, Flute, and you'll shortly have all you need to know about farming, whether in your own head or in the heads of others. What do you say, Devon?"

"Would you pay me, Mr. Cable?"

"Devon!" gagged Da.

Cable was chortling, though. "Course I will, if I'm satisfied. What sort of country would we be living in if a man didn't get paid for his sweat? Get yourself over to my place tomorrow and we'll put you to the yoke."

Devon nodded eagerly, his dark eyes shining. Cable touched his hat to Mam and Audrey, switched the horse, and trundled away. Mam and Da stood watching him go and though Caffy's hand was fastened to Mam's skirt and tugging it urgently she wasn't taking any notice of him, and Da was stripping his nails to the quick.

Devon started early because Cable's property was well away from our own, past the nearest town and a fair distance after that. Mam fitted him with a pair of Da's cut-down dungarees and packed a crib of stew and a spoon, and his only other luggage was the shirt he was not wearing. He was buzzing round the shanty before dawn, raring to get going, and I could guess why. He could see Champion, that pony, coming magnificent and snorting into view. We didn't know how long Cable would keep him but Devon said he wasn't coming home until he had the money to buy the animal that galloped through his dreams. I was bitter at the prospect, knowing he'd never let me so much as touch the thing, hearing already the skiting.

Mam and I walked to the road with him and waited until the rabbito's cart came over the rise.

Mam tried to help him onto the tray but he shook her hand away and sprang up by himself. He was thirteen, and easily insulted. "Be on your best behavior," she told him, and Devon hung his head because her words had made the men sitting beside him snicker and nudge.

It would be a long day for Devon: when the cart reached the town he'd have to start walking and when the shade was lengthening in the late afternoon Da said he would probably be arriving at the gate of Cable's homestead with the whole day's journey smeared across his face. Caffy cried, missing his brother, and Tin crept out of the underground, but he wasn't a consolation. Caffy shrieked at the sight of him.

"The baby doesn't know Tin," Audrey said quietly. Tin had vanished again, maybe gone as far away as the tunnel would let him, but we were in the habit of speaking low when we didn't want him hearing something, because we'd been caught out before.

"No," said Da.

"He's been under the house for all of Caffy's life."

"So Caffy won't miss him. You don't miss what you've never had. Caffy won't grow up feeling any loss."

"I miss Devon," I announced, but no one seemed concerned; Mam passed me a plate of dripping and damper and Audrey poured the tea.

It was me who spotted Devon first, early evening a week later, trudging toward the house, and I dropped the firewood and went charging down the hill to meet him, whooping out his name. It was only when I was near enough to see his face that I came sliding to a standstill and my words stuttered to a stop. Never had I seen anyone look so downcast as he.

He went inside and flopped in a chair and we all gathered around. Caffy tried to climb his legs but Mam plucked him away. "Devvy?" she asked, and Devon burst into tears, just like that, as if the sound of her voice sprung a tank behind his eyes. He was ashamed to be crying, being as he was thirteen, and he hid his face and kicked his feet in angry misery. Mam told us to take the baby and go outside. As soon as the door was shut behind us, Da and Audrey and I pressed our ears to the slab. We couldn't hear clearly, but we heard enough to make Da swear. Devon said that Cable had given him an hour's instructing and then made him go out alone, wiring fences from the break of day. But Devon wasn't as strong as the work needed him to be, and he hadn't had the practice that would make him do it well. Cable had sent him packing without paying him a penny. Audrey's eyes were shooting sparks— you could see it in the gloom.

"You should talk to Cable, Court." Mam whispered it late that night, when she expected Audrey and me to be sleeping. Devon was out on the veranda, hunched up in his blankets, and I could hear his husky, exhausted breathing.

"It's best to leave it. What's done is done."

"But it's dreadful for Devon. I'm sure he tried his best. Maybe, if you explained things to Mr. Cable..."

I heard the bed creak as Da shifted his bones. "It's a lesson for him, Thora. You shouldn't expect life to be fair. My father taught me that, went out of his way to teach me that. He's never kept a single promise in his life, that man."

"Let's not talk of him—"

"When I was young he used to bet me a shilling I couldn't hit a ball over a fence and when I did it, he'd say the bet only held if it had been a fast bowl or a googly or whichever it hadn't been. He'd say he would bring home something good to eat and when he returned with nothing, after I'd smacked my lips all day, he'd say he never stated which particular day he intended bringing something home. And if I dared complain, he would give me a clip and tell me life wasn't fair."

"There's fairness, and there's cruelty. Being cruel to a child simply teaches it to be cruel in its turn."

There was a length of silence. Then Da said, "Cable doesn't have any little ones, does he? He lost that boy with the influenza."

"And his wife."

"Life hasn't always been fair to him, either."

"Life's not been deliberately cruel to him. Life isn't like that—only people are. I'll go and speak to Mr. Cable myself, tomorrow."

"Don't be silly, Thora." There was a pause—I wondered if Da was gnawing his nails. Eventually he said, "I'll make the man see sense about the thing."

I thought I'd never get to sleep with the worrying but when I woke up next morning Da had gone and Devon was under the house with Tin.

Vandery Cable's homestead was set in a garden of tangled brier roses that had grown for four generations of Cables and that's where Da had met him, amongst the flowers and black-spotted leaves, hearing in the distance the low rumble and alarming shrill of the swine. Only Cable had come out of the house but Da could see Cable's station hand loitering watchful at a window. It was dusk, and a silken wind nudged the brim of Da's hat until he took it off as Cable sauntered down the steps toward him. Then the breeze frolicked through his hair, mussing it in his eyes. "Where's your heart, Mr. Cable?" is what Da asked the pig farmer.

"Right here in my chest, where it's always been. Why do you want to know?"

"You owe my son a week's wages."

"That's what he told you, is it?" Cable laughed open-mouthed; Da caught a whiff of sherry and saw gold. "You should know better, Flute, than to take the word of a boy, having been one once yourself."

"I hope I've raised my children to tell the truth."

"Then Devon must have told you how I lost two good breeding sows through his sloppy workmanship. That's my reason for keeping his wages, and I'm running at a loss even doing that."

Da scraped the hair from his eyes. Cable's hair wasn't bothered by the breeze, having been oiled into a glistening cap. He smiled beneath this shell. "Don't tell me you didn't hear about those sows," he said. "Walked clear through one of Devon's baggy fences, both of them, and I haven't seen a hair of either since. Salted up in someone's ceiling by now, I'd reckon. It's a miracle I didn't lose the herd."

Da muttered, "No. I didn't hear that. I'm sorry for it, Mr. Cable."

"So am I. You can understand why I had to let Devon go. I want fences that will keep the creatures in, not let them out."

"He hadn't had experience—"

"He got the same teaching everyone gets and all anyone should need."

"As I say, I'm sorry. He's just a lad, Mr. Cable, not skillful, and it's likely his attention wandered. He was hoping to buy a pony with his earnings here. He's been saving for years."

"I'm not a charity, Flute, nor is my heart the bleeding kind. I'm a landowner, a man of business. To me and men like me, poor work equals poor pay. Would you pay for a job so shabbily done that you lose two quality head of swine?"

"What I'm saying is—"

"No!" Cable barked. "Answer the question, Flute. Would you reward a man for work so shabbily done?"

Da wrung his hands in silence, buckling his hat. Cable's mouth twisted.

"Go home, Court," he said. "Don't speak about this to me again. I tried to do your family a favor and came out the worse for it, and there's some that would say I've a right to demand from you the price of those hogs, but I'm not asking. Having this conversation with you, however, is tempting me to change my mind."

Da had thanked him for his time and set his hat on his head. As he limped away down the cart path, he could feel Cable's eyes tracking him all the way to the gate.

"I did everything anyone could, Thora," Da told Mam late that evening. "There was no talking sense to him. No matter what I said, he was going to sneak his way around it. He shouted me down; I couldn't get a word in edgewise. He deserved the spots knocked off him but what could I do? Nothing, not with his man standing like a dog at the window."

Mam didn't say a word; all Tin and I heard was the rasp of the bedframe do the sighing for her. In the floorboards beneath the bed, Tin had found a knot that could be pried loose and slotted in again, and when it was out you could hear through it just like you can see a room through a keyhole. Mam didn't speak, because there was nothing for her to say. Tin laid his face on the earth and the moon-light snaking under the house was pooled in his eyes so they glowed at me, clear and cool.

After that night no one said another word about Da's visit to Vandery Cable, and because I knew Da would throttle me for eavesdropping, I could never mention what I heard and had to play dumb. It meant that I could never ask him why the story was such a strange one, why it was like two mirrors standing opposite each other and spangling reflec-tions—why it was that, when you considered it one way, Devon was the hurt and injured party, but if you viewed it from the other angle, Cable had rightness on his side. I looked from one mirror to the other until my neck cricked, and I still couldn't puzzle it out. All I could do was what everyone expected me to do, being eight and ignorant. I took Devon's side and made the insult legendary; the name of Vandery Cable was spoken with a snarl upon my lips.

Devon never mentioned his pony again, either: his dream had curdled. He took the coins he had painstakingly saved and spent them all at once, not on anything he could keep but on a jar of boiled sweets. In the weeks and months afterward he grew morose and malcontent, as well as tall and spotty.

Mam became concerned; Mr. Murphy said it was doubtless his age. Devon would sit for hours on the veranda, with the hem of his trousers riding high on his calves and the sleeves of his shirt unbuttoned on his arms, stroking a dog's ear and never wanting to do the things we used to do. He would not come exploring, knowing as he did every leaf and stone of the land. The ghost of the miner was not wafting through the mineshaft so there was no point concocting spells that might summon it and put it in our power. Making statues from the creek clay was childish and boring, and, disliking black-berries, what reason would he have to get torn and sticky collecting them? Why would he want to do any of those things, seeing as how he'd done them already a thousand times before? "Go away, Harper," he would say, turning his eyes from me.

The only other thing that happened, after Da visited Cable, was that Tin suddenly started digging for all that he was worth. You'd hear him when you woke in the night, scratching and burrowing. You could hear the dogs crowding him, their solid bodies jostling, their tails thumping the floor. You would hear him getting farther away, quarrying through the earth much faster now, striving for his safety.

Summer passed and autumn came and with it came rain, the first we had seen for a year and a half, sometimes heavy and sometimes light and sometimes just a mist on your face as if you'd walked through a cobweb strung between trees, but always, always there. Caffy was scared of it and would shake his fists and bawl; I cavorted in the puddles and got drenched to the bloomers trying to teach him bravery. Soon he, like me, only found the rain a bleak thing, and we stared from the windows like sad prisoners behind bars. I watched the water drain off the earth through cracks that had opened during summer and I began to feel nervous. Falling ceaseless, the rain seemed to be falling with a purpose. Once there was water enough, something would surely happen. The last time it had rained like this, the creek bank had collapsed on Tin. I watched for him, and worried.

One afternoon we spotted Art Campbell hurrying toward the shanty with his hands clamped on his head, bowed like a grass blade by the rain upon his back. Mam pulled the door and he made for the fire, jiggling and shedding water. "Is something wrong, Art?" she asked, as he did his vitus dance and we gawped at him bug-eyed.

"You're as bad as my Gert, Thora," he said, struggling out of his jacket while his feet beat the boards. His naked cheeks and scalp had turned a heated shade of pink. "A fella can't get a bit energetic without a woman assuming the worst. That's right, eh, Court?"

"The only thing I've ever seen twitch the way you're doing was a mutt that knocked open a hive. Have you been stung?"

"Worse than that! You can keep your mutt, I'm more of a cat and can't abide my feet getting wet. They were wet from the start of the war till its ending and I promised them I'd never let them get that way again. Pah, imagine what winter will be like, if it's this bad already. The road's a bog and in town they're talking about flooding. Here," he said, handing Da a damp envelope. "This was waiting for you at the dry-gooder's, and I knew I'd be passing."

Da took the envelope and I saw his name written there, the words smeared by its journey with Mr. Campbell. We children clustered as he opened it because we rarely got letters and this was exciting, but Da shielded the paper and would not let us see. Mam was finding a cloth for Mr. Campbell and hanging his jacket near the fire, but her eyes kept flitting to Da. "Audrey, Devon, Harper," she said sharply. "Let your father have the light. Arthur, I'll make a pot of tea."

"My father has died," said Da. "He's dead and buried a month."

It made the room go quiet and we heard droplets splat from the cuffs of Mr. Campbell's coat. Mam said, "Oh, Court."

"Ah, I'm sorry, Court. I wouldn't have come in carrying on so theatrical if I'd known the news was bad."

Da didn't look up from the letter. "You weren't to know, Art. My father and I haven't spoken for a good while, anyway; I'd be a hypocrite to go weeping and having hurt feelings."

"Is it our grandfather, Da?"

"Of course it is, Harper, idiot—"

"Hush, Devon." Mam had hung the kettle in the

fireplace and was adding twigs to the flames, though the fire was already blazing and it was a waste of kindling. "Is that all the note says, Court?"

"The estate needs to be settled. The lawyers want me to go to the city."

"What's an estate?"

"Harper. Does it say what needs to be settled, exactly?"

Da shook his head. "Just says it needs doing."

"You'll have to go."

"Hmm."

"Oh, Da, can I go too?"

"Will there be much to do, Court?" asked Mr. Campbell. "I mean, was your father . . . a man of means?"

"He never went hungry," said Mam. "There's a house."

"My mother's jewelry."

"Other bits and pieces. Furniture."

"You got any brothers and sisters, Court?"

"No. My mother was taken when I was the little one's age. There's only myself."

Mr. Campbell nodded, biting his white cold lips. Da and Mam were gazing at each other. The kettle was bubbling ignored. "God bless him," said Mam suddenly. "God grant him rest."

"Aye. May he rest in peace."

Da folded the letter and slipped it into the envelope. "I'll make a start tomorrow morning."

Mr. Campbell kept on nodding, as if something had unsprung inside his scrawny neck. "Best not to keep these things waiting," he said.

An estate is what the dead leaves behind and the living gets to keep. During the three weeks Da was in the city, Mam told us about the house our grandfather had lived in, how it had an upstairs and a downstairs and a staircase bent like an elbow linking in between, how it had windows back and front so some rooms got light in the morning and some in the afternoon, and how it had a space in the ceiling where Mam had lived with Audrey and Devon while Da was fighting the war. Devon said he wished he had a room like that now, way up hidden in the treetops, and I asked what room I could have, if Devon got the attic. Mam said I would probably have to share a room with Audrey because the smallest room wasn't good for anything but a nursery and Audrey groaned on hearing that, as if she were being tortured. Mam said there was a kitchen with an oven big enough for piglets and if she was missing an ingredient there was a store half a mile down the road where she'd send me with a list. There was a table that had chess squares laid into its surface and Devon said if he had a table like that he would learn the rules of playing the game and Mam said Da could teach him. Thinking of teaching made me think unwillingly of school and Mam said there was a convent for young ladies that would take ten minutes to reach on foot and it was a very different school from my own, with hats and stockings and lessons lasting all day, even if the teacher got sick of our faces. I worried that none of the girls would be friendly to me, coming in as I would a stranger, but Mam said I was bound to find someone who would pity me. Audrey suggested we might need new clothes to match a life so glorious and Mam said we could all get new clothes for the city, because country clothes would not do. I looked at the dogs and said we'd have to find homes for them because it would be no good taking them with us and Devon asked then, "What about Tin?"

"Tin will come too," Mam said, but I could tell by the way she said it that she had forgotten all about Tin—forgotten to give him a room in the house, forgotten to send him to school and buy new clothes for him, forgotten to carve his share of the piglet. "Don't crowd me so, Harper," she said, and pushed me away.

"Tin couldn't dig in the city," Devon decided. "The ground is covered with stone. There's cobbles and drains that would get in his way."

"Tin will come with us," Mam said sourly.

When Da came home we pounded down the hill to meet him and we hung off his arms as if he were the key to that house with the elbowed stairway. He took Caffy from Audrey and ruffled my hair. "I've missed you all," he told us, and I gazed up eagerly into his coal-colored eyes. Three weeks in the city, in that wonderful house, three weeks near the school and the store just along the road, should have made him different—I dreamed it would make him sparkle—but he looked just the same, save for his hair's mourning trim. All of us were biting our tongues against our questions, because Mam had told us to let him tell it as he wished. Even so, she couldn't help asking, "How did it go, Court?"

"There was more to be done than I expected."

Mam's hands were clasped so tight that her fingernails were going white. "Such as?"

"All the furniture had to be sold."

She blinked, her hands went still. "Sold?"

"He had debts. I was surprised. I always thought he was pretty careful that way. No doubt that's where my mother's wedding ring went. His own was gone."

"What about the chess table?"

"That went in the auction. It brought a fair price." Da frowned, and turned to Devon. "How did you know about that?" he asked. "I'd forgotten the chess table."

"I've been telling them about the house," said Mam.

Da was carrying Caffy and walking slowly up the hill, his clean black boots squelching through the mud. "The house. That's another thing I believed wrong about. I always thought he owned that house. He never said a thing to make me think otherwise. Can you believe, he was renting. Renting, and I never knew. He was a crafty old bugger; he never let on about things like that. Always kept his cards close. Always wanted to appear grand in the eyes of others."

No one said anything so I asked, "It's our house now though, isn't it, Da?"

He beamed at me. "We've got a house already, chicken. What would we want with another?"

"But—aren't I going to the school? Da?"

"Harper, you've got a school—"

My heart started thumping. "But—what about us going to the city? Da? Da, Mam said we were going to live in Grandda's house—"

"I didn't, Harper. I only told you what it was like there. Don't tell such lies."

I swung to look at her, but she wasn't looking at me. She wasn't looking at Devon or Audrey, who were staring at her too. She was looking at the sky, at nothing, her dark hair blowing across her face. My eyes were filling with tears, so I put my hands over them. Mam said, "Well, that's done with, anyway."

"Yes. It was a fiddlesome business."

"And he's well buried?"

"I saw the grave, left orders for the stone."

"Good," said Mam. "Good."

"There was a few quid left over, after everything was done."

I peeped over my fingertips at this, but Da had turned to Devon. "It's to go to you, Devon," he said. "That's what the will stated, that anything left over was yours. It's not much, but it's something."

Devon's jaw lolled. "Is it enough to buy the pony?"

"I reckon there's enough to buy the pony."

Da had brought the money home in his swag, a pile of notes locked safely in a flat carved wooden box. There seemed enough to swim in, I thought, but Da said that was just my unaccustomed eyes. He said that someone used to seeing money would say there wasn't much at all but that if Devon was careful, he'd find he could make it spread pretty well. "Save it," Da advised him. "Get your pony, because you've been busting your gut for that, but save what remains. That's the wise way of doing things."

Devon couldn't hold that box tight enough. He let me sniff the money but not feel it. Da went to sleep with the juice of his dinner still on his lips and Mam turned the lantern down low. I washed the plates in the basin, the nails of the floorboards nipping into my knees, and listened to Devon prattle. Mam mended by the lamp's light, patching Da's raggy shirtsleeves. Audrey was ironing in silence, and even Caffy was sitting dumb. It was only Devon who wasn't aching like he'd taken a bait.

"Course color doesn't make a difference, but I believe I'll get a chestnut. I was wanting a gray, but now I think a chestnut."

"You want a healthy one, that's what."

"True. A saddle and bridle, I can get them secondhand. I don't think the horse will mind, long as the tack's comfortable."

Audrey smacked the iron on dampened cloth; you could see the steam roll through the air.

"We'll need a yard for him, so I'll start building it tomorrow, and somewhere to keep the feed. And I'll save what's left over, as Da said. There might be a day when I want something else. I reckon there will be, probably."

He hugged himself, excited; Mam licked the cotton and rethreaded the needle. "Yes," she said, "you've had the last laugh on Mr. Cable. You got your horse without him, after all."

Audrey snorted fiercely, pressing the iron home hard. "Grandda didn't even know Devon," she said stonily. "He should have left that money to Da. At least then we wouldn't have to listen to that blockhead's bragging."

"It was Grandda's money," Devon said hotly. "He could leave it to whoever he liked."

"Hush, you'll wake your father. Devon's right, Audrey, it was Grandfather's money, to do with as he chose."

"Well it was mean of him and it isn't fair. It isn't fair to me or Harper or Caffy or Tin—"

"What's not fair? Why would Tin or Caffy need money?"

She slammed the iron on its heel and wheeled to hiss at him. "It's not fair because now you can get what you want, Devon, but we won't be getting anything. Things are staying just the same, for all the rest of us. Da will go out trapping rabbits tomorrow, and that hole in Harper's shoe will be letting in the rain. Mam will be wearing that same old dress and she'll give Caffy half her dinner so he's got the food to make him grow. So go and spend your money, Devon, and I hope you enjoy doing it. Just don't tell us about it, that's the favor you can do for me."

Devon pressed against the wall, clutching the box in his lap. "You're being spiteful, that's all."

"Haven't I the right to be? Wouldn't you be?"

"Let him alone, Audrey," Mam sighed.

Audrey swung toward the fire, her blue eyes sparking flames. Caffy was sniveling at the raised voices, I dashed my hands and scooped him up and huddled, with him, between the legs of Mam's chair. It bothered me, what Audrey said. The hole in my shoe let in water but I was used to it and it would dry out at the end of the rain. Mam's dress, I thought, was soothingly familiar as the touch of her hand; she shared her meals with Caffy because he was too clumsy for a plate of his own. Da trapped rabbits because that was what Da did—that was his calling and place in the world. These things had never seemed wrong to me, and it troubled me that Audrey thought another way. Audrey was clever—cleverer than me—and sometimes she knew things that I didn't know. I chewed my lip thinking and, with Caffy quelled and Devon petulant, the room was silent except for the flames. Then Devon asked, "Why did Grandda leave the money to me, Mam? Why didn't he give it to Da?"

"Your father and grandfather disagreed."

"What about?"

Mam lowered her mending. "A disagreement isn't always about a particular thing. You know how, when you come across something that makes you queasy, you avoid that thing as best you can? The two of them felt that way about each other."

And then she told us how Grandda had been a clerk who'd always expected to be made something more prestigious and how he secured for his son, Da, the job as junior clerk so he would know the man he was boss of, when the company moved him up and away. But the company didn't move Grandda anywhere, not sharing the old man's dreamed-up destiny; more galling was the trust they put in Court, the capable, when it should rightly have gone to Grandda. And Grandda hated it, and seethed over his mistake. When war was declared Grandda told Da to enlist, but Da did not want to. He was a married man with a baby, and hordes were volunteering, anyway; there was no call for an underweight thing like him. But Grandda kept the subject simmering, reading aloud the headlines every day. Volunteers started to die overseas and dwindle away at home. Grandda encouraged and hounded, saying the company didn't need Da but the nation certainly did, saying the child on its way would be born safely without him lurking, saying it was a privilege to be given an opportunity to fight and go, hurry, go. Still Da refused and Grandda said the bones of the dead were crying out for vengeance, Mam and Audrey and the not-yet-born baby could live in the attic of Grandda's house and he would take proper care, the army was begging for anyone now, married or single, old or young, and did Da like it, behaving like a coward? Did he like making his father look the coward by having a coward for a son? People, he said, were whispering, and soon would come the white feather blown in under the door. "Your own children,"

Grandda warned him, "will forever hang their heads in shame."

So Da went to France, where the mud was, and realized, when he got there, that his father had sent him away to die.

Inside I felt all knotted with rage. "He should have come home—Mam, I wish Da had come home—"

"But he was a long way away. Too far to come home."

"He should never have listened to that horrible man."

"Hush up, Harper, you don't understand."

Mam had written letters to him, cheerful letters finished off with crossed kisses telling him of new-born Devon and Audrey's first sentence and her lovely flaxen curling hair, never breathing a word of how Grandda growled at the sight and sound and smell of children or how he judged Mam's housekeeping slovenly and her childrearing faulty and begrudged every scrap she put in the little ones' mouths. In three years Mam never wrote a word of complaint, posting her letters faithfully each fortnight and praying he received at least some. But she remembered things, for later.

All throughout those years the company kept

Grandda pinned in his lowly position and now and then made mutterings about the strength of his memory; when Da returned in one piece from the war, Grandda knew his days at the company were numbered. A bullet wound in the foot would not stop a young man from doing sums. So when the government offered land to the soldiers as a signal of its great gratitude, unused land that should with industry become sprawling prosperous farms, Grandda started singing his old tune. The country life is a splendid one for children and Da would have fellow-feeling for his neighbors, them being soldiers, too. Don't get sunk in the same pit as your father, Grandda cautioned him: don't spend your life thanklessly drudging for others, as bullied as a mule in the shafts.

Da didn't trust Grandda as far as he could boot him, but he wanted to go. He'd come home sickened and sallow, the endings grated from his nerves. The country sounded like salvation to him, like rest and finally refuge. He and Mam had been apart a long time, and to his children he was a baffling stranger. In the seclusion of the countryside, they could recollect one another in peace. But more than that, Da wanted to see with his own eyes a place where ruined specters did not loom, to walk on earth that was not spiked with bone, to breathe air that did not reek of blood, to see birds scoop unhurried through unbroken empty sky. Together he and Mam took up the offer of settlement and from the first they were thankful for the shanty and the kindness of the neighbors, for the relief and serenity. It was only later they remembered that they had never been farmers.

Audrey said, "And Da and Grandda never spoke after that?"

"They knew each was a blight on the life of the other. Occasionally there was a letter, but they never saw each other again."

"I will never stop talking to you, Mam," I said stoutly.

Mam smiled and ran a hand over my head; her hands were made of the toughest skin, and snaggled in my hair.

The next morning Devon gave the box and the money to Da. His chin was quivering and he kept shifting so the floorboards creaked beneath his weight but his words came out clearly, clouded only with the cold. He must have spent the night planning what he was meaning to say.

"Mam needs a new dress," he said. "Harper needs new boots. Other things, we need. Maybe some things to make a farm. A proper farm, I mean, with crops and animals. You said this money would spread pretty good if it was spent carefully. I don't think there's enough for much, but we could make a start. One day, we could have a better farm than Mr. Cable."

Da said, "That money is yours, Devon."

Devon hitched from one foot to the other, awkward and overgrown in his too-short clothes. His arms were sagging under the heft of the box; his pale cheeks were blotched and his look kept sliding away. "I want to give it to you. I can do that, can't I? I didn't know Grandda, and I didn't earn that money from him. I mean—he never gave me trouble in my life—that's what I mean."

Da's gaze went to Mam, who was leaning watching in the door. "No," he said. "I don't suppose he gave you much trouble."

"It doesn't matter about the pony. There's other things we need. I'll get a pony another day."

You could see it almost strangled Devon to say it, that he had to wring the words out of himself, that it made him weak at the knees. Da took the box and stared at him. I thought he should be happy but instead he just seemed sad. "That pony of yours," he said. "That's the first thing I intend to buy."

So the rest of us stopped at home while Da and Devon were gone three days, spending in the town. The wait was exciting, Mam was laughing and I was rowdy and even Audrey joked and played. But when the pair of them came home, there was no cloth for making dresses, and there were no new boots for me. There was a cage holding two aggravated chickens and there was a tall gray horse for Devon and, astonishingly, there were three hefty

Red Poll cows. I remember Mam standing stock-still in the yard while the creatures milled, heads hanging, her skirts weighted with a hem of muck and her voice scarcely rising above a whisper. "Court," she said, "what have you done?"

"It's all right, Mam," said Devon, his voice twanging nervously. He was holding the reins of his horse and it was a fine horse, but his face was bright with shame.

"Look at them," Da said, waving at the cattle who were sniffing at the mud. "Aren't they beauties, Thora?"

Mam looked him over slowly, as if her last hope was that he was hiding the things she wanted to see. Da tried to lift the head of a heifer so she could admire it but the animal grunted and pulled away. Mam's lip curled.

"We needed to plant a vegetable garden. We needed seeds for a crop."

"But where's the sense in growing crops when beef cattle grow themselves? That's what I started thinking."

"We needed blankets for winter. All the children need shoes."

"And we will get them. In a year or two, when these cows—"

Mam clutched her hands in her hair and Devon cringed against the horse's chest. "A year or two?" she cried. "A year or two! My God, do you think we can go without blankets and boots and Lord knows what else for another whole year or two?"

"We've survived so far, Thora, and we'll survive a while longer—"

Mam caught my collar and brandished me at him. "This child hasn't had a new piece of clothing in her life," she said. "Her shoes are tied up with string. She hasn't a coat to keep the weather out of her. You'll remember that, Court, for your *while longer*, won't you?"

Oh, she was ropeable. She shook me and I flailed inside my dress, my tiptoes scraping the ground. Then she turned and marched into the shanty, swinging fast the door. We stared after her but she was gone and there was nothing, as if she'd never been here, and Caffy started instantly to cry. Audrey hoisted him out of the mud and I reached for her free hand. Devon looked at Da. "I told you," he said. "I told you!"

"She'll come round," said Da, but I didn't think he sounded sure. "She'll be pleased in a year or two."

We hobbled the cows and the horse and left

them to graze the high land, and set up a wire for the chickens just beyond the kitchen door. Da sat outside until evening, watching them, sipping whiskey from a flask. That night, when I crept under the shanty to hear him and Mam talking, there was the quiet of the grave. I looked out into the moonlight at the dark shapes of the cattle, at the lean gray browsing horse. I wished, suddenly, that Devon could have done the skiting I had been dreading for so long. With the horse should have come the bragging, the two happenings twisted like twine, but what Da had done had soured every-thing, and nothing was as I'd imagined it would be. Poor horse, I thought, how can Devon love you now, poor thing. Tin touched my ankle, passing me the knot from the floorboard. I plugged it into place and then lay for the longest time without moving, against the freezing earth.

It was wet and sludgy that winter, just as Mr. Campbell had forecast it should be, and the soles of Da's boots would be baubled with clods when he came in from rabbiting, the kitchen wood had to be dried near the fireplace before it could burn. The road to town was washed out for almost a fortnight and Clarrie Gaston, who was as dippy as a scrub tick from being kicked by a dray, was dredged drowned from the creek and his wife was putting on her weeds when Clarrie sat upright and asked for tea. But the sludge and the water and the sheer coldness of the days couldn't hold Da at the shanty, the smallness of which kept it warm; the beef heifers wanted a large fenced-off roam and Da was busy attending to it, a handful of neighbors arriving each day to help him. Jock Murphy, who had a natural talent for authority though Da said he was just a boilermaker before the war, issued directions because Da hadn't built a fence before; Devon was always in Murphy's shadow, watching and listening and jumping to commands. It was Jock's idea that they strip the beams that lined the gold mine, scrub down the wood and knife out the decay, and use these strong pieces as posts. Tin came up to watch their progress, blinking in the daylight and wrapping himself in his arms. Winter in the underground had turned his skin a snowy white, but his clothes had stayed good and dry. Billy Godwin, the greyhound man, tried to talk him into digging the postholes but Tin only smiled vaguely, having none of that. For the railings the men cut bush timber, felling the few tall trees that had been left standing when the land was cleared long ago, and chiseled the wood by hand. From the scraps they made the gap-faced shelter and the neatly closing gate. It took weeks for the work to be finished and when it was the fence swept a graceful circle behind the shanty, and it looked magnificent. "Have you ever seen anything like this, Harper?" Da asked me proudly and I said no, because I hadn't. The land, for miles round where we lived, had once been a single and enormous crop property and it had not been fenced, there being nothing movable in need of closing in; fences were a rare sight still, although the land had a dozen different owners now. "No one has a fence as grand as this," said Da, and lifted me so I could stand on the top railing and have a broader view.

"Every time you see this fence, chicken, you remember what it means and how special it is and how lucky you are to call it your own. No fussy and weedy old crops for us! Beef's the way to go, you'll see. We'll be the envy of everyone, chicken."

But when Vandery Cable came around sniffing, he said otherwise. Da and the neighbors stood silently while he cast his eye over the cattle. He leaned on his hands and gave the fence a violent shaking. "That should hold them, eh, Devon?" he said. "It's nice to see you shifting yourself, Court, but what, exactly, are your intentions?"

Da squared his shoulders and stepped forward. "Build up the herd until—"

"Where's your bull? All I see is ladies."

"I'm hoping to borrow one, to begin with. I'll put the word around."

"I hope the word travels. You'll find nothing nearby that suits your wants, I'm telling you now. What fool told you to buy into beef?"

"No one told me," said Da. "I decided for myself. The stock agent said—"

"The agent said! I'll bet he didn't say, *You look like an easy touch, I'll offload these heifers onto you.* Didn't I tell you to put a crop in, Flute? I remember doing so. Did I ever mention beef to you? No. If you'd asked my opinion before going off halfcocked, I would have told you not to touch it. If you'd asked Jock Murphy his opinion, I'm damn sure he'd have told you the same. Red meat has never thrived in these parts. Look at the place: it's green now but this isn't usual, it's typically scabby and bone-dry. Come summer again and your cattle are going to be eating dirt and filling up with flies. You'll have to buy feed if you want to keep them healthy, and have you got the means to do that year after year? What about water, eh? That creek's a hike away and it's a trickle at the height of the year—you'll need a well or a dam if you don't want your stock drinking air. I swear, it's giving me a headache just thinking about it—why didn't you stop him, Murphy, when you heard what he was up to?"

Mr. Murphy was denting the earth with his heel. "Things might not be so bad, Vandery. It's done now, anyway, so we have to make the best of things."

Cable scoffed fiercely. "These animals are going to bring you nothing but grief, Flute. I'm sorry to say it in front of the children, but there it is. If any of you others are thinking about going into beef, take the advice of a farmer and plump for something else. I'll take your advice when I need to know anything about soldiering."

Da and the neighbors stared at their feet. Mr. Cable pushed off from the fence, tossing words backward as he went, "I'll ask around anyway, Court. See if I can flush out a bull for you. Someone might know someone who keeps one as a pet."

"That's decent of you, Mr. Cable."

We watched Cable's jinker jamble away and

stood saying nothing. Art Campbell was stretching his braces and letting them snap back to his chest again. Da shook the fence, as Cable had done, and didn't say what he was thinking. Then, "Things might not go so badly," said Jock Murphy, "as Vandery made them seem."

"That man ain't got a generous bone in his body," said Mr. Osborne, and spat over the fence. "He thinks no good about anything but something of his own."

"He knows about farming, though," said Da.

"Thinks he knows everything, is what he does. Who knows everything? I bet there's plenty he's yet to learn."

"In summer," said Mr. Murphy, "if you let the cattle wander, they'll find enough grass to keep going. It won't be the best feed, so you won't get the best meat, but at least it won't cost you anything and the beasts will stay alive."

"There you go, Court!" Kindly Mr. Robertson, who had been still and very pale, burst into sudden life with tumbling, hopeful words. "What does it matter if the meat isn't the best in the world? Which of us is so grand that we can only have the best? I know I'm happy with something flavorsome and filling, I don't need it melting on my tongue. In fact, I'm happier if it's got a bit of chew to it. You know you've eaten, then."

"I'm willing to taste your cattle, Court," said Mr. Campbell. "Beef is beef, far as I'm concerned. I don't care what it's been eating before I start eating it."

"That Cable's a green-eye, is all," said Mr. Robertson. "He'll be herding a hundred head of beef before the week's out, you'll see."

"But we'll only buy from you, Court. Cable can keep his green meat, I say."

And they talked on like that, standing in a circle smoking cigarettes and grinding the butts into the churned-up ground, until what Vandery Cable had said didn't worry me any more than a crow would, passing overhead. But Da must have listened to what Cable said, or maybe Mr. Murphy did some friendly advising, for near the end of the winter Da announced that we were sinking a well. Mam brooded on the cost of it, Da swore it must be done. Mam said the cattle seemed to need a lot, considering they were only cows. The well-sinker came with his broad corkscrew and drove it deep into the earth, coming up dry the first time and having the same thing happen again. Smiling into the man's damp face, Mr. Murphy said casually, "What about that mite of yours, Court? If anyone knows where the water's underground, I reckon it would be him."

"Fetch him, Harper," said Da.

I hollered down the tunnel for Tin and after a time he appeared, Devon's old shirt reaching to his bare knees and the cuffs hanging past his hands. He stood in the drizzle while it was explained what needed doing and the drizzle stripped the color from where it touched his face and legs, leaving behind a streak of white. The well-sinker stared suspiciously and rather fearfully at him, clutching his auger close, while Da did all the talking. Tin wasn't dancing with eagerness to be helpful but he did what was asked of him, hunting about and eventually tapping the dirt in the shadow of the fence, a place some distance from the first two holes. The well-sinker declared himself doubtful but he dug the probe because Da was insisting that he do so, and promising he would pay. The auger, it didn't need to go deep before it came up dripping, and I leaped off the fence with glee. Tin had disappeared by then, knowing all along he was not mistaken. The well-sinker looked after him, wrestling with peevishness and awe.

• • •

Once Mam let up cursing the sight of the heifers and we resigned ourselves to owning them and were even proud of them, despite what Cable had to say, Devon did not feel so badly about showing off his horse. No one had ever taught him to ride but he turned out to be a natural, he sat a saddle as if he'd been glued. Champion was better than a pony; he was a full-grown horse, and when I pressed my cheek against his warm gray chest his ears, pricked upright, turned and quivered high above my head. He was in disposition a gentleman but he would kick up and spring about to please Devon, and pretend to be half brumby. He was about ten years old when he arrived at our place, and someone had treated him cruelly in those years; he had scars on his flanks and a mouth so hard he couldn't be guided anywhere he didn't decide to go, but he never misbehaved for Devon, whom he loved. He would pluck his bridle from its hook and rattle it to catch his master's attention and together they would rove the district for hours. Several times Champion came to the door after dark and stood waiting patiently until Da dragged sleeping Devon from the saddle.

One day I was watching Devon brush the horse

down, sleepy myself in the evening air. It was spring, I remember, and the earth was warming, already being dry enough for me to lie upon. The horse was smacking his lips and rippling his coat with each sweep of the brush. Devon was speaking to him and I could hear him distantly, a purr floating through the haze.

"You're the color of the moon, aren't you. You're a good horse, a wild horse, a dangerous mad-eyed horse. You can fly. You fly like a bird. You're an eagle horse, you are, a wild-eyed eagle demon horse. You're as tall as a tree and strong as a mountain. No one is faster than you, you can thrash them all, you could do it on three legs . . ."

He knocked the brush clean on a post and the noise roused me, blinking. "Champy can't understand you," I said blearily. "Why do you tell him how special he is, when he can't understand you?"

"He can understand me," said Devon gravely. "He understands everything I say. Don't you, Champ?"

Something made the horse wag its long gray head and although it must have been a fluke, maybe his mane tickling his ears, it looked like Champion was agreeing that what Devon said was true, that he could indeed understand. I took a fancy to believing that he could, anyway. I was nine years old, still young enough to believe as I pleased.

The world you live in when you are nine is different from the world that other people live within. My home was my empire and the only place that mattered and I never gave a thought to other empires beyond the horizon, so I couldn't understand why Mam and Da seemed so concerned when Billy Godwin, back from the city near the end of that year, told them that the stock market had collapsed and there was too much coal and that the price of wheat and wool had dropped like a stone. I didn't know what a stock market was and I didn't see how too much coal could be a bad thing, coal being something we never had. The price of wool and wheat shouldn't matter to us because we were farming beef. Things seemed good, to me. There were endless rabbits for eating, Devon had his longed-for horse, and the heifers had made it through the winter unscathed by Cable's jaundiced eye. So I didn't understand why Mam and Da and Mr. Godwin should be interested in things happening so far away and sit up discussing them into the night. I didn't understand that something was coming like a tidal wave around the earth and that we had no hope of outrunning it; nor did I know that the only shelter we had to protect us from the worst of it was what we owned that night and nothing more. And when the shanty collapsed one breezy December morning, I did not know how bad that was for us until Da raised a hand and slapped me across the face.

Devon, Audrey, and I were walking down the hill when it happened, on our way to school. Audrey was carrying a handful of books but Devon and I were swinging our arms with nothing. Devon was saying he planned to ride Champion to school when classes went back after summer and I was seething at the idea of him disappearing down the road because I knew he would never let me climb up behind him, never. I'd be forced to walk all the way alone, given this was Audrey's last year of having to go. Even now she was helping the teacher more than she was trying to learn. I was picturing myself walking lonesome and unaided, choking on road dust and staggering with snakebite but reeling gallantly on, and I was almost in tears of pity and admiration when the noise, behind us, made me whirl.

For a second, nothing looked changed: the clouds were still floating and the trees were still crooking and the ground was a patchwork of silver-green and brown, shoots of new grass squeezing past mattings of old. But the noise had been terrible, as if someone had taken a hacksaw to the sky, and a hundred birds were screeching and dashing madly from cover, so it hadn't been our imaginings. And then, it was as though my eyes were wrong, rather than what I saw. The shanty was tipped at an angle. I tilted my head to balance it and for a moment this worked. Then the roof of the house tore through the center and the room where we slept and ate and did most of our living vanished—vanished as if the earth had eaten it, and planks went flying like the ground was spitting out bones.

Audrey screamed at me to get Da but it was Devon who took off running; I sprinted up the hill after Audrey. Mam and Caffy were standing at the clothesline, Caffy with his hands clamped to his ears and Mam staring stupefied with Da's Sunday shirt dripping in her hands. The roof of the shanty was lying on the earth like a hat blown from the head of a giant and although there were bristles of wood standing up around its edges, the walls appeared to be gone. Pressed kerosene tins and strips of corrugated iron were thrown all around and in the roof you could see holes from where they had been. What was left of the veranda was groaning and shuddering, its stumps pulled clean from the ground. The wall of Mam and Da's bedroom had been peeled like the lid of a fruit can and the hem of the bed's drapery was frippering in the breeze; in the midst of the bed was a great dirty smear of grit and more was showering down. Everything was moaning and snapping and tumbling, the whole house cussing and swearing. The chimney, though, stood sturdy, and the fire burned serenely below the simmering kettle. The sight of it made me blink, it being so strange.

Suddenly Da and Devon were there, Da laming along on his gammy shot foot and letting out a yell on seeing things close for the first time, and smacking a fist to his forehead. He stepped forward until his boots touched the roof and then he knelt and stared through a hole left by a loosened kerosene tin. Mam told us to be careful and we went to look, too. With the sun risen over my head and pouring down its rays, I had a bright-lit view. The walls of the room weren't folded up between the roof and the ground, as I had expected. Rather, opened up beneath the roof was a cavernous space, and the walls were scrambled about within it. The room had fallen in, not fallen down. It had fallen into Tin's domain.

"Where is he?" Mam whispered. "Lord, Court, where is he?"

"Tin!" Da shouted. "Tin!"

There wasn't any answer; we heard a piece of iron tapping and waterfalls of dirt drizzling into the hole. The heifers had bolted at the noise and were still trotting nervously around their paddock, the screeching birds had spiraled away. The dogs stood quivering on the slope of a mullock heap, shame-faced as though they were to blame. I looked down into the broken room, at the earth spuming up like lava. The floor was snapped in a thousand places, made choppy as the sea. The table and chairs had been knocked higgledy-piggledy and the cupboard and beds were kindling. Everywhere was a scramble of plates and pots and blankets and clothes, filthy and buried in shards and dirt. Most of the walling had collapsed, the slabs sliding over one another and buckling into the room or smashing, the jagged breaks like devil's hands. If Tin was under there, he was dead for sure.

"Tin!" I piped. "Where are you?"

"Tin," Mam said—but not loud, and nothing else. It was the forlornest word I ever heard.

And then he appeared, framed in what was left of the window. I didn't understand how he could crouch there, in a space where no space should be, but later I found out why. When Tin had dug his first tunnel, he hadn't been making for the earth's core. He'd only gone down a certain distance before changing direction, and changing it many times; he'd excavated an ant's nest, with passages veering everywhere. It was the earliest passages, the ones woven beneath the shanty, that caved in that morning, and because they were many and some of them were vast, they'd left plenty of space, once flattened, to accommodate the room. And it was the passages that had saved him: he'd been down one of them at the moment the collapse happened, and perhaps quite far away. He could appear at the window and have space enough to crouch because behind him a tunnel slithered away.

Da must have guessed this straight off. I expected him to shout with joy at the sight of his pet alive, but he did not. Instead he squawked, "Tin! Damn it, look at what you've done!"

"Court, you'll frighten him. Come out, Tin, it's treacherous—"

"Get here! You plurry well get up here, Tin, and see what you've done!"

"Da," Audrey breathed, "don't, don't say that; be pleased, Da . . ."

Tin hadn't moved, or shifted his gaze from Da. He didn't look at the rubble and I knew he had seen it already, that he'd been watching everything. "Tin," I said gently, but he didn't glance to me. His eyes, on Da's furious face, were furious in return. Cats when cornered look the same. He wore nothing but a pair of cut-down tatty trousers and he crouched, taut and coiled: had he a tail, it would have lashed. While Da yelled Tin was motionless but the moment Da slouched and dropped his head in his hands Tin did what a cat does, given the chance to escape. Rather than run, he retreated with caution, stiffly haughty, disdain wafting like smoke after him. Mam called to him hopefully, craning between the roof's sharp torn edges. "Tin, it's dangerous—please come out, just for today?"

"My God," Da was groaning, his fingers in his eyes.

"If you won't come out, then go far away. Go away from the shanty, to where you will be safe . . ."

"Oh my God, what next? What next?"

"Tin . . . Tin, listen . . . go far away . . ."

Mam swept her hair from her eyes, searching for him a final time. He was gone, though, and she sighed. Da's moaning made her look at him. "There's no point taking on," she said. "What's done is done."

But Da didn't drop his hands. "Merciful Mary," he was mumbling. "Mother of God."

He was hurting himself—I could see his nails were biting into his skin. I hurried to him and tried to pry his hands away. "It doesn't matter, Da," I chirruped. "It's all right now. We'll build a new house, a better house, you'll see—"

"This is what it is," he said, talking over me. "I'm an educated man and my house is in the ground."

Mam stood up, shaking the dust from her apron. "Devon," she said, "run for Mr. Murphy. We will need his help."

"No!" Da barked hoarsely. "It's my house. I'll fix it myself."

"It's our house, Court. It belongs to me and the children. Devon, go."

Da grappled at his scalp, rocking drunkenly. "All my life it's been one thing after another. I have an education, I used to go to dances, all I want is to be left alone—"

"Da!" I squealed, pawing at his arm. He was cutting into himself and it was making me want to cry. He tried to shake himself free but I clung all the tighter. Devon was standing riveted, uncertain whether to go or stay, and Mam and Audrey were speaking angrily, not to each other but at me. Caffy, forgotten, let out a heartbroken sob, and the tears spilled from my eyes. "Da," I begged, "stand up!"

"Damn it," Da was chanting. "Damn, damn, damn."

"Harper," Mam warned, "come away!"

"Don't say that, Da, please don't worry—"

"Harper! Devon, I told you to go!"

"We can fix the shanty, we can fix it today—see, Da, the chimney is good, the chimney didn't fall, it—"

That's when he slapped my face. His hand came up and slashed across my cheek and nose. Devon said later it must have been an accident—Da's arm, when he moved it, must have flown through the air mistakenly or maybe I moved it myself, and made it go askew—but I knew he only said it to console.

Da slapped me, and it hurt; it made me hit the ground like a sack. It made Mam rush forward and roar. "Don't you do that!" she screamed. "Don't you hit that child!"

I thought this was strange, even then when I was plonked in the dirt and my brain was reeling, because Da smacked me often, whenever I was rebellious, and Mam never took offense before. This time, however, she hauled me to my feet and, with her free hand, slammed Da over the head. "Don't you take your miseries out on a child," she snarled. "You're a coward, you are, taking on like an infant. Do you think you're the only one living this life? You aren't. The children and I didn't ask for this. Get to your feet, you disgust me. That house needs rebuilding, and you're going to start doing it today."

Da was on his knees, tottering. "With what?" he cried, over Caffy's petrified wailing. "How do you intend I fix it, Thora? There's nothing left of it! It's firewood!"

"Go to the mill and buy timber!"

"Buy it with what? They don't give the stuff away!"

"You've spent it all, have you? Every penny of your father's money."

"Don't fight, please, Mammy —"

"And what should I have done with it? Money's meant for spending. The fence, the well, none of those things were cheap."

"— Dadda —!"

"You are such a fool."

"Oh, it's foolish to look to the future, is it?"

"The future!" Mam tossed her head scornfully. "Three mangy cows — is that our future? Three mangy cows, which Cable says are worthless, anyway? God help us, Court, that's all I can say!"

"I pray He hears you, because those cows are all we've got now!"

I was sobbing helplessly, clutching the folds of Mam's skirts. "Stop it!" I bawled. "Stop fighting!"

"I was trying to do my best, Thora," said Da. He staggered unstably to his feet and stared around blindly. "I was only trying my best. That was wrong of me, and I'm sorry for doing it."

"As am I. You can't imagine how sorry." Mam hoisted Caffy and sponged his snotty nose. "I'm taking the children to Rose Murphy's, and they won't be coming home until there's a decent home for them to come to. I don't care how you do it, but you'll find the means to right this mess. Sell the cows and pull down the fence and do whatever else you have to do. Taking on like a baby, ah, you revolt me. Audrey, Devon, Harper, come, we're going."

Audrey tried to lead me away but the sight of Da standing by himself agonized my heart; I didn't care if he slapped me a thousand times, I wanted us to stay with him. I struggled against Audrey and bellowed for my Da but Mam gripped my wrist and between her and Audrey they carried me along, the tears cascading down my cheeks, my face still smarting, craning to see over my shoulder for one last glimpse of him, and it wasn't until we were a mile or two along the road and trudging in miserable silence that the image of Da standing abject and abandoned was dimmed in my eyes, for a moment, by the memory of Tin in the window, run completely wild.

Mam made me mop my face as we got nearer the Murphys', and told me to put a smile onto it. Mrs. Murphy warmed cocoa and Mr. Murphy joggled Caffy on his knees while Mam told them about the shanty. "Of course you can stay here," said Mrs. Murphy. "You know you don't need to ask. Where's Court, now?"

"I told him to come along but he wouldn't, he wanted to stay. He wants to make a start on things as soon as he can. You know how he is; he knows his own mind. I'll take a plate over of an evening and he'll be dandy."

Audrey, Devon, and I stared dismally into our mugs. Mr. Murphy said, "Must have been a bit of excitement, eh? Not every day your house falls down. It'll be the rain we had over winter that did it. Ground got sodden and then—splat! Tin was lucky."

"I told you there'd be trouble, having that villain under your feet." Mrs. Murphy was nodding, satisfied. "Didn't I tell you, Thora? Imagine it, tunnels going everywhere—what did you expect would happen? Thank the stars no one was inside at the time, or we'd be digging for the lot of you."

"Tin didn't mean it," Audrey said softly. "He's only a little boy."

But I just felt sick at the thought of Tin. I remembered Da hitting me and Mam hitting Da and them roaring at each other and how terrified I had been. I was limp and exhausted and in my throat was a hard knot of fear lest my Da think we didn't love him anymore. And it seemed to me that Mrs. Murphy was right, and that Tin was to blame. I looked inside myself and knew I wouldn't care if I never saw him again.

Mam took a meal over for Da and Tin at dusk, making us stay behind. That night we slept together in the Murphys' spare room, Mam and Caffy in the bed and me and Devon and Audrey on the floor. In the moonlight edging past the curtain I could see the glint of Mam's eyes, traveling the patterned ceiling.

"Mam?"

"Hmm."

". . . I'll sell Champion. We'll have some money, then."

Mam didn't look away from the ceiling. "No," she said. "You keep the horse, Devon."

I looked at the ceiling too, and my thoughts flew like witches around Tin. I remembered how like a cat he'd looked, how his eyes had filled with a wild cat's rage. Let him be wild, I thought: let him be wild like a snake, which disappears at the tremor of footsteps. Let me never see him again because of what he's done; let his diggings take him to the end of the dirt.

Life was tedious at the Murphys'. Mrs. Murphy had a stockpile of chores that she was too timid or swollen to do, and after school Devon and I would always be up some ladder with a cloth and bucket or bent over double attending the skirting boards. She would box Audrey and me in the kitchen and break open her recipe books; she said we'd never regret learning to cook, but the kitchen was sweltery and the only thing I took into my head was that butter creamed with sugar is a delight to tongue and eye. The Murphys were slightly well-to-do—Da said that Mrs. must have come from money because Mr. surely didn't, what with the boilermaking history—and while she stirred and measured, Mrs. Murphy talked constantly about some fandangled ice chest she'd seen in a magazine and was persuading her Jock to buy. In the late afternoon we would be freed from slavery and Devon would run to find Mr. Murphy in the fields but there was nothing diverting for me. Murphy land was planted land and dreary for it, with no stock to tend or creek to splash or impressive trees to climb. I would sit and stare mournfully homeward but never dared set out in that direction— Mam said she'd skin me if I tried. She went home every evening, ferrying vitals for Tin and Da, but she never let me go with her. Sometimes she would bring back flowers that she said Da had picked for me. I missed Da, and used to press the flowers for mooning over in private. Da was camping in the animal shelter, Mam said, because the bedroom was unstable. The nights were warm and the animals kept him company, so he wasn't minding it. She said she never saw Tin, that he wouldn't answer to her calling, and that sometimes his dinner tray was licked so clean it must be that the dogs had got it in the night. "Aren't you worried about that child?" asked Mrs. Murphy, and Mam replied, "No, Rose. He has what he wants."

One of the few things that broke the monotony of those slow drifting days was spying on the Murphys and the piddling chair. The piddling chair stood in a corner of the Murphys' bedroom looking ordinary and modest but it had a padded seat that lifted to reveal a porcelain bowl underneath, secreted from view by a fringe around the well-built legs. Mr. and Mrs. Murphy used the chair when they needed to go at night, saving them from picking their way to the outhouse with a candle. As soon as we heard a rustling, Devon and I would glide from our bed. We'd cross the hall like lizards and peep around the frame of the Murphys' bedroom door. There'd be Rose or Jock, nightdress up and perched or nightshirt up and wobbling. It would be all Devon and I could do not to writhe about, wracked with revolted hilarity.

It was Mrs. Murphy on the chair when we'd been there a fortnight but Mr. Murphy was awake, too, and they were chatting quietly. Mr. Murphy went to see Da most days and when he returned, he'd say, "We put the spire on the palace this morning," or "Tomorrow we'll be fitting the stained-glass windows." We knew he was teasing but he would never say anything that wasn't that way.

Now Mrs. Murphy, on the piddling seat, was saying, "The man doesn't deserve your help, if he's saying such things to you. The rudeness. Who does he think he is?"

"It was the grog he had in him, Rosie. You can't take offense when it's the drink speaking, not the man."

"You're too good to him. Most people are too good to him, I say." Mrs. Murphy creaked on the seat, and concentrated a moment. "Bless my heart," she murmured, and then asked louder, "So nothing has been done?"

"Like I say, most of the rubble is still in the hole. Manpower isn't the difficulty—there's plenty who are willing to chip in. It's Flute who's the problem. He sits on his rump mouldering and won't give any answer regarding what he wants done. If I suggest a thing, I get a tongue-lashing, like today. No, I've never seen a man take a setback so hard. He's never without his flask of scoot—he was well into it when I got there this morning. Gets tetchy with it, too."

The musty smell of piss was rising in the air. "That's good of him, washing the few deeners he has down his throat, with no regard for his responsibilities. Drink's brought many a family to ruin. Thora hasn't said a word, though you'd reckon she'd know what's going on. Ashamed, no doubt, as you would be. Something has to be done."

Jock turned his weight heavily. "Aye. But you can't build a house from thin air, and what's left of the place you wouldn't get a kennel from. He's got no choice but to trade the cattle for bits and pieces, but he's refusing to do it. I'll have his mind changed eventually but I want to get them housed before the bottle gets the best of him, that's my only concern."

"Maybe they should all go underground, like the youngster."

"Haw."

Mrs. Murphy closed the seat and hedged her way to the bed. Once she was in beside her husband she said, "I don't mind having them here, it's companionship. But they can't stay forever. Those children have appetites."

"What you do for your brothers, you do for the Lord."

"Maybe, but it's here on Earth that we have to eat."

Devon and I waited until we were certain they were asleep before creeping to our bed. I wanted to talk to Devon but he turned his back on me. When I touched his arm he jerked like he'd been bitten, and curled into a motionless ball. So I lay silent, feeling the floor beneath me, cold and heartsick with worry. I fretted about my Da, that Da would make Mr. Murphy so angry he would decide not to help us, that we would have nowhere to live if that happened, that nothing would be good anymore.

Next morning I clung to Mam, lurking in her shadow and irritating her with a glum face and damp eyes, but when I wouldn't eat the jammy bread we got for breakfast she surmised I must be ill. "Are you ailing, Harper?" she asked, and I nodded fraily, because I felt that I was. She said I could stay home from school and even that gave me no joy.

I was lying in her lap when Vandery Cable arrived at the Murphys' wanting to see her, and she made to send me away. But, "Leave her be," said Mr. Cable. "There's nothing I'll say that's unfit for a child to hear."

So Mam held on to me and she and Mr. Cable smiled tautly across the room. The morning sun was beaming in the windows and you could see a fog of dust motes floating around him, surging if he moved. His wing collar was starched sharp and straight as the line of his nose. Mrs. Murphy brought in a tray of tea things and went out again reluctantly and when Cable shook his head as Mam offered him a sandwich, not a single hair fell out of line. "I won't keep you longer than I have to, Mrs. Flute. But I thought it best to come here, to yourself, rather than to your husband. I've heard about what's been happening."

Mam lowered her look, smoothed a ruckle in my sleeve. Mr. Cable's gaze dipped to me; I thought he was going to speak to me, for he opened his mouth — but shut it again suddenly and instead turned solemnly to Mam.

"I'll be brief. I've a hay barn I'm not using and not likely to use in the future. If you can arrange for pulling it down and shifting the timber, it's yours."

Mam paused. "That's kind of you, Mr. Cable, but

there's no need. Court is selling the beef cows back to the stock agent and we'll be fixing things that way."

Cable shuttered his eyes. His eyes were—his whole face was—dark and shaded and watchful, despite the sunlight coming in. "Mrs. Flute, I fear you'll find your hopes frustrated. The agent won't buy those cows for the price he sold them. I've my doubts he'll take them off you at all."

". . . Oh."

"I believe you already suspected as much."

Mam didn't answer, stroking my cheek with the back of her hand.

"The barn would suit your purpose."

She was staring at me emptily and it made me fidgety. "We do need timber, as you say."

"Your husband should see his way to accepting the offer."

Mam nodded, at me. "Yes. I'll speak to him. He'll accept gratefully, I'm sure."

"If he finds that difficult, tell him to consider it a favor, not a gift. Tell him I expect something in return one day."

"That's the wise way of putting it, I'm sure, sir."

The pig farmer stood, clutching his hat. "You're a woman of sense, Mrs. Flute. Good day."

He gave a stiff bow and went for the door but stopped when Mam asked, "What shall we do with the cattle, Mr. Cable?"

"Keep them," he answered instantly. "There's hungry times coming."

With that, he left, bobbing another bow before closing the door.

For the two weeks that followed I didn't get off the couch where I had been lying, that morning, with my face in Mam's hands. I became ill through and through, as if Vandery Cable had brought something contagious with him when he entered the room. I had visions, when I was feverish, of this deadly thing crawling from his mouth. He hadn't opened it to speak to me, he'd opened it to release whatever it was that slithered in under my eyelids and swam around my body, blighting my limbs and bones and brain. For two weeks I lay prone, shivering when I was not sweating. I slept and mumbled in my sleep and had knotted, peculiar dreams. In my dreams I saw Da loom over me and held up my arms for someone who rippled away. I saw Tin and called his name and he turned to me a face distrusting and whiskery. I saw bizarre concoctions of people and animals. I saw Mr. Cable many times, the contagious thing scuttling behind his teeth. I was never so sick that anyone prayed for my soul but I was fragile enough to be left where I lay, tormented enough to be querulous, needy enough to have Mam sleep on the floor beside me. I had no strength, through those days, to care for anything anyone told me. Words littered the floor around my couch and during the worst of it I could hear them jawing and wanted the breeze in, to scatter them away.

And then, one morning, I felt a spring of the couch gouging into my spine and knew I was getting better. I sighted, as if from a faraway hill, the child I used to be. A day later I could sit up and nibble; the day after that I walked wonkily to the outhouse, being ashamed, when healthy, to use the pail.

Feeling better, I regretted those words I'd been deaf to, and hankered to hear them again. I knew things had been happening that I would have murdered to see. I was by myself and stranded, with only the impatient Mrs. Murphy to answer my questions, and I listened to what she said like the religious to a gospel.

"Devon went home a week ago, he's camped in the shelter with your Da; the lice he'll have caught, I don't know. Your mother and sister and the little tyke left three days ago, as soon as the roof was put down. Phew, my girl, it's time we got you in the tub. Shift yourself, you reek."

"And is Mr. Murphy helping with the building?"

"Well, he's gone from dawn to dusk doing something, that's all I know. No, listen: every man in the neighborhood is doing what he can to get your family on its feet. There's work going on every minute of the day. Your father, he's miserable over not being able to pay them, but payment's not what they want. People like to help each other when they can. That's a ludicrous grin you've got on, girl, you look like a loon."

"I'm happy."

"Gone mad, is more like it. Your mother was determined you had the meningitis, you know. I said, *You've not seen meningitis, Thora, if you picture that's how it looks.* Myself, I think you saw there was exertion on the horizon, and you were canny enough to plead infirmity."

"Oh, no, I wasn't pretending! I would love to help with the building!"

She tweaked my chin. "I know you would, dear, I was ragging you. Sit up so I can plump your pillow. You'd be in heaven out there, getting under everyone's feet."

"Have you seen the new house, Mrs. Murphy?"

"I haven't, but I've seen the dust of it in Mr. Murphy's clothes. I imagine it's as handsome as a house can be."

"And big?"

"Well, there's a good amount of wood in a barn. You'll have to wait and see."

I scowled. "How long do I have to wait?"

"Until the waiting's over."

"But I'm missing everything," I sulked. "I missed out seeing the barn get pulled down. I'm missing out seeing the house get put up. I'm missing everything!"

"Boo hoo. You shouldn't be such a germy thing, then, should you."

"I want to go home!"

"That's gratitude, you little gobshite."

"I miss my Da."

Back she shot, "I hope he's remembering to miss you."

Two long days later I was freed: Mr. Murphy put me on his shoulders and carried me, high-strung as a kitten, home. I was expecting to see something grand, of course, believing a hay barn could be fashioned into a palace. Trapped on the Murphy couch, my imagination had been the only part of me able to ramble as it pleased. Mr. Murphy stopped when the house came into view, and pinched my toes. "What do you think of that, Harper?"

I stared and stared. The house was small, but it was glittering. It was flashing, like water going over rocks in the sun. "It's twinkling," I whispered. "It's twinkling and shining."

I wobbled on his shoulders as he laughed. "I said we were building you a palace, didn't I? What good's a palace if it doesn't gleam like gold?"

"Hurry," I urged, kicking him on. "Hurry."

So he gripped my ankles and together we charged up the hill.

The house glittered because the wood it was made from had been polished for half a century by straw, which had left behind it not only a deep honey gloss but also its smell, sweet, and heartwarming. On some of the planks you could see the dents of pitchforks jabbed by boys who would be men now, or by men who would be old. You could see their writing, figures scrawled in chalk as they'd counted off the bales. You could see where they had taken out their pocketknives and shaved the planks when idle and bored. But mostly you could see the shine of all that straw, blinding at sunset, glorious at dawn. The new house was a palace.

It had four rooms, three of them larger than any room I'd ever lived in, while the fourth room was a sleepout for Devon and tiny, tucked away and made from the remnants of Mam and Da's bedroom.

Stout cyclone-wire beds had been built for each of us and even for Caffy, as well as a kitchen table and chairs. In every room was a window with neat-fitting shutters and the gaps between the planks had been stopped with gobs of clay. The roof was made of corrugated iron, with no patching of kerosene tin. The chimney had been pulled apart and rebuilt in the new kitchen, and given a glassy stone hearth. The clothesline had been propped near to the back door, and the outhouse was being moved closer. There was a veranda that was broader and longer than our old one, and if I stood on it and levered on my toes I could see where the shanty had been. There was nothing left to say it had stood but a shallow dust bowl in the hill.

Mr. Murphy had guessed that the earth around the shanty was riddled with Tin's early tunnels and was precarious for it: but, not knowing the range of Tin's work, he'd looked at the ground and real-ized none of it could be counted on, there was not a hand span's worth that might not crumble unex-pectedly into itself. So he'd marked up the rockiest patch of earth he could find, reasoning Tin would have avoided such obstacles, and the house had been built there, a hundred paces from where the shanty had been. I went to the dust bowl and inspected it but the ground had been churned, topped up with mullock, and walked over too often; there was not a stone or a scratch I could recognize. I thought about the times Tin and I had lain beneath the shanty listening to conversations we weren't supposed to hear, the cool breeze licking the soles of our feet and a dog beside us, its chin between its toes. I had liked it that I was the only one small enough to squeeze down there with him; I had liked it that he trusted me enough to climb from the tunnels and stretch alongside me. The stumps the new house stood on were so low that a rat would have to suck in its breath to get by. The new house had rocks beneath it, meaning Tin shouldn't have been in its vicinity in the past and was discouraged for the future. From where I stood I looked for sign of him or his doings but our land seemed the same as anybody else's.

I flew to Da as soon as I saw him but he was holding a flask and two borrowed glasses and he kneed me aside. "Careful," he said, "you'll break things. Feeling better now?"

I put my hands where his knee had knocked my stomach, smiling dazedly up at him. I wanted to throw my arms around his knees, to dance with the excitement of seeing him again, but I reckoned he would think that was childish, flapping about in front of everyone. The house wasn't perfectly finished and the neighbors were fussing here and there, tapping things with hammers. Da gave me the glasses to carry and I skipped beside him proudly. "Have you seen Tin, Da?"

"Not a wink, chicken, but I've been too busy to be doing any looking."

We stopped at the new outhouse, where Mr. Godwin and Mr. Robertson were nailing boards around the pit and Godwin's slinky greyhounds were flattened in the sun. "Bill," said Da, "Harry, take something for your thirst. We're out of glasses, Izzy—will the bottle do for you?"

From behind the outhouse stepped a young man I'd never seen before, who thanked Da politely before taking the bottle. He wore a creased clean pair of dungarees and the tip of his nose was burned and peeling. He had the bluest eyes, the creamiest skin, the most magnificent shock of scarlet hair that I had ever seen. When he put the bottle to his mouth, a dribble of beer escaped his sun-kissed lips.

"I'm Harper Flute," I said. "I've been sick at the Murphys'."

"Not on Rosie's best rug, I hope," said Mr.

Godwin, and cawed. They'd been drinking, I could tell. "Introduce yourself to the lady, Izzy."

"Hello." The young man smiled at me, showing teeth polished as stars. "I'm Izzy Godwin. I'm sorry about you being sick."

"Izzy's come out from the city, Harper. He's come to toughen up. One day he might even be as tough as you! No good wafting through life like a china doll, is there? You're not a china doll, are you, Harper?"

"No, I'm not, Mr. Godwin."

"You don't even own a china doll. Probably never seen one."

"She's got a stake in three Red Poll heifers," said Da. "That's worth fifty dolls."

The men laughed and I laughed uncertainly with them. Izzy was gripping the bottle by the throat and smiling, his elegant eyes examining the ground. "Show Izzy your heifers, Harper," said Mr. Godwin. "He's never met one close before."

"Aye, go on, Izzy."

I took his hand gladly, leading him past the gate and into the paddock, smiling beatifically up at him all the time. The cows saw us coming and lifted their heads, chewing on thoughtfully. "How long are you staying?" I asked.

"I don't know. My father said things wouldn't be too bad in the country for a while. He asked Uncle Bill if I could stay. Keep me out of mischief and all."

His hand felt frail and silky in mine, so invitingly crushable that I couldn't help giving it a squeeze. "What mischief do you mean?"

"Oh, you know—the lads, and all."

The heifers had lumbered forward to meet us, blowing foam from their nostrils and trailing ropes of drool. I grabbed one by the underjaw and said, "You can pet her, she won't bite."

The cow switched her tail and Izzy dodged backward, but caught hold of his courage and ran his fingers along the animal's spine. He said, "She's not so soft as I thought she'd be."

"She's got hard bones inside her."

"Long eyelashes. She smells nice, too. Clean. Nice, she is."

He stayed there skimming his fingers over the velvety hide of the cow and I stood beside him grinning like a mooncalf, witless and utterly smitten. Most people I knew, I had known from the minute I was born: the sight of him, so creamy and new, made my heart fair pound. I asked, "Um, how old are you?"

"Seventeen. How old are you?"

"Ten," I said, because I would be, eventually.

"Ten. That's grown-up."

"It is," I agreed.

My plan was to stop with him for the rest of the day and I would have, had not Audrey appeared when I was showing him the chickens and told me that Mam needed me in the kitchen. Mam knew nothing about it, though, and when I came out Audrey and Izzy were gone and only chickens were in the cage.

So began a rivalry between me and no one, for to Audrey I was naught but an irritation. I cursed the fact that I'd been ill and given her a head start of days alone with him while I lay captured on that flowery couch. Izzy was living on the Godwin property, which was just along the road from our own, and he wandered over most evenings with his pockets full of interesting things for Caffy and me, smooth stones or peg dolls or mouse skeletons. I'd belt down the hill to meet him and hold to my heart his milky spider of a hand. Everyone said he was making eyes at Audrey but I reckoned it was she making eyes at him: whenever they went out strolling together, it was always her suggesting that they do. Da insisted that Devon or I should stroll with them because that seemed right and proper; Audrey stormed about this law, although not in front of Mam or Da. Once we were beyond sight of the house, however, she'd do anything to yank the thorn from her side. Devon was an easy bribe, being always on the back of Champion and itching to gallop away to where the local boys were waiting for him, but I was trickier to budge. I could clamber onto Izzy's shoulders while we wandered the paths and scratch my fingers through his blood-red hair and nobody but Audrey minded; I could clown about and play chasey with him while Audrey had to sit prettily, demurely gnashing her teeth. She was nearly sixteen, but she primmed about like a full-blown lady. I had always been a degree frightened of her, although I loved and trusted her and usually looked upon all she said or did with a reverence. When we were out in the paddocks with Izzy, however, tormenting her became my favorite hobby. I would not disappear for anything less than a sack of lollies and even them I'd gobble as fast as I could before hurrying out of the scrub. Occasionally I was quick enough to see her hand resting on his, or her brow tilted close to his lips. She'd spring sideways when she saw me coming, and Izzy would flush crimson.

One night I was watching her brush her hair before she went to bed, her corn-colored locks spilling in curls to her elbows. As well as clever and wise I thought she was beautiful, like a princess in a story, and she saw me staring at her. "Harper?" she said.

"Yes?"

"Izzy lets you stay around because you're a child."

I frowned past the hem of my blanket, confused. "So?"

"So," she said, and lowered the brush, "you shouldn't think that he likes you, when all he's doing is taking pity on a child."

"He does like me. He never wants me to go away. It's always you who says I have to leave you and him alone."

"He's too polite to say what he really thinks, I told you. And you have to stop giving him flowers. He throws them away, you know."

". . . They wilt. He has to throw them away."

Audrey sighed, and looked at me loftily. "You have to do as I say, Harper. I'm going to marry him, after all."

"Really?" I sat up and gawped at her. "When?"

"After we get engaged."

"Oh, Audrey! Have you told Mam and Da?"

"No. And don't you tell them, either. And don't say anything to Izzy."

"Doesn't he know?"

She flipped her hair forward and brushed its underside. "He's shy," she said, behind this veil. "You'll embarrass him if you say anything. It's a secret, and I'm being kind telling it to you. So don't you breathe a word."

"I won't. Golly, Audrey."

"And you must leave us in peace, sometimes, when we go out walking. He won't ask me to marry him while you're standing about goggling. If you're good, you can be my bridesmaid."

I had that same feeling I was getting more and more as I grew older, a feeling like I was trying to see through a fog or reach for something my fingers could touch but not wrap around. I didn't know it then, but I was starting to realize the world is not one place, but two, and that you move from one to the other only with the years. I was living mostly in the first world, but I had a toe dipped in the second. The tip of a toe doesn't tell you much, however, so I believed what Audrey said to me.

Through autumn and into winter I waited impatiently for her and Izzy to get married and if Audrey looked at me sideways when the three of us were walking, I hastened to hurry away.

Devon rode Champion to and from school that year and when he was in a good mood he would double-dink me and the saddle would dent into my legs, but I didn't mind. The weather growing cold showed up the faults in the new house: boards in the floor warped, the shutters swelled and let the moths in when they wouldn't close properly, and my bed squeaked when I rolled. Da tended the cattle and walked them on long forages for food; for us he went on snaring rabbits until he came home from town one day and Mam looked at the money and said, "Where's the rest of it, Court?"

"That's all I got."

"You drank it, didn't you?"

"No, Thora." Da sat at the table and his thumbs circled his temples. "That's all I was given, I swear. They're saying skins are fetching nothing now, it's not worth the trapping. The fellow was decent in giving me that; he said not to bother coming back again."

Mam picked up the coins one by one and studied

them in her palm. She said, "We've still the children to feed. It's still worth the trapping."

"I know it."

"And when the taste of rabbit chokes me, we'll be eating beef."

Da looked dour and said nothing and I shrank into a corner with my sponge and bucket, sudding the floor distractedly. I had that peculiar feeling again, that reaching, foggy feeling. Da loved the heifers, and Mam knew it. Her heart was getting hard.

During winter we had strangers come to the house, two or three of them every week, who would brave the growling dogs and knock timidly on the wall. These were shabby men who had traveled miles and were often dripping and drooped. They would apologize for the nuisance and drag off their hats and they never came inside if there was mud on their shoes. They had small things they were selling, notepaper or ribbons, boot blacker or pocket Bibles. Some of them would smile tenderly and say they had a son Caffy's age or a daughter of mine, left home in the city with its mother. Mam never bought from the men but she would give them a plate of soup or a handful of boiled eggs. If they were drinking men Da would pour a glass of the liquor he stored in the keg, and if they were soldiers he'd sit and reminisce with them on the step. Devon once muttered that he didn't like these travelers, being beggars with trinkets as they were, and Da clipped him so swiftly that Devon hit the wall.

We never saw Tin, though I kept my eyes open everywhere. I had wished him to the end of the dirt when the shanty fell down, and I started to fear he might have heard. I put my lips to the earth and whispered that I hadn't meant it, that that terrible day had passed as all of them do, but it didn't bring him home. I stood and stared at the golden house and wondered what he'd thought when he'd seen it was built on rock, that he had no choice except keeping away.

And then one night there was hammering at the door and Da opened it to Vandery Cable looking liverish, his hand at the scruff of Tin's slender neck. "I caught this thieving from my beehives," he said, and shoved Tin into the room. Tin stumbled forward and stopped where the fire stained his flesh orange and made his eyes squint and look stung. He was wearing a coat of scrappy rabbit that had gaps where the pelts didn't meet. They were not skins from our own racks, for they were peppered with shot holes. Being a thief he was destined to be caught but you could see that Cable hadn't done the catching. Where rabbit paws dangled at his thighs, Tin had the bleeding wounds of dog teeth.

"I've done a fair amount for this family," said Cable, his glare scouring each of us in turn. "I didn't expect to have my hives raided as thanks. If that boy eats what's left of the honey, what are the bees expected to live off until spring? Can you answer me that? Can you?"

We could not; Da said, "I'm sorry. I'm very sorry, Mr. Cable."

"If I lose my swarm, then God help you, Flute!"

"I know—I'm sorry—the boy goes where he pleases, he does as he likes, he won't hear a word from anyone. He's no respect for his mother, he's got no family feeling. I know you've done plenty for us and we're grateful, Mr. Cable. No one can say we aren't grateful. Tin—now Tin, say you're sorry."

Tin considered the pig farmer; then he shut his eyes and yawned.

"Tin!" Da screeched. "Do as you're told!"

And the strange feeling came to me, like sucking cold air. I knew that although Tin had been Da's pet and favorite, Da would flog Tin to his knees if he thought it would please Vandery Cable.

"He's sorry," I said hotly. "Tin is sorry."

"Sell him to a circus," said Cable. "You'll get a good price for him."

He turned then, and left, and we heard the whip strike the rump of the jinker horse and the animal's shrill whinnying.

Having Tin in the room was like hosting someone you've heard about, but never met: I was delighted to see him but I couldn't think what to say. None of us crowded him, because you never crowd something whose next move you cannot guess. His gaze prowled the room without pausing, not restless, I thought, and not curious, either, but as if watching were his habit. He was clasping and twining his fingers, the stickiness of the honey bothering him, and flecks of beeswax were clinging to his rabbit skins. "If you were hungry, Tin," said Mam, "why didn't you come here? I would have given you something to eat."

She filled the basin with water and though he did not seem to feel the bites, Tin let her patch them up; he wouldn't let her brush his pelts, despite their crust of dirt. "Stay with us," she begged him, "just for the night. Wouldn't you like a warm bath? Don't you want to sleep somewhere soft? Let me

wash your hair and clean your face, oh Tin, why
won't you?"

"Leave him, Mam," said Devon quietly.

Mam wrung her hands, defeated; Tin was standing by the door with a look of studied patience,
like a dog when it wants to go. So Da let him out,
and in a glint he was gone.

"Tin!" I cried out, startling myself. Without a
thought I jumped up and ran into the darkness, and
almost ran into him, for he'd stopped and waited
for me. He stood still, only fiddling and clenching
his fingers, his chin tilted to look at me. He was
tiny, and I had grown.

"Tin," I said, "don't go. Don't go so far away.
Don't go to Mr. Cable's—how will I find you, if
you dig so far away?"

He scuffed the dirt and smiled quickly, meaning
nothing by it. He wasn't listening, he didn't care.
"Tin," I beseeched, "bring your digging here.
Come home—come closer to home. I look for you
everywhere and I never see you anymore."

I hung my head, because I couldn't say things
the way I wanted to. Tin was watching me, but he
was only waiting. I turned and went back to the
house. Mam was standing at the door. She called to
him to keep his leg clean, to rinse it in the creek

daily, but he had vanished in the pitch and she said to herself, "I don't suppose he heard." He didn't hear, I reckoned.

But a few weeks later I found the rags she'd wrapped around his wounds, lank strips of cloth snagged in the grass quite close to home. It made my blood thump and I sniffed about like a hound. I couldn't see anything to prove it but I knew I was right, inside. A tree sprouts a branch and ants add corridors to their nest and Tin was carving a new tunnel because I'd asked him to come home. He was coming as near to the house as the rocks would let him. I shouted, and carried the rags in triumph to Mam. There was no blood on them and they signified Tin was close; I thought she would be happy, but she didn't look that way.

She didn't burn the rags, as she would have done if they had been mine. She folded them into a little case and over the next few years she added to the case any remnants of Tin that she could find. His baby clothes didn't go in, for they had been worn by Caffy—what went into the case had to be Tin's and his alone. She cut a lock of his hair once and that went in, with a ribbon tied around it. Besides that, hardly nothing.

Mam was boiling the laundry, that's why she wanted us to take Caffy. He was a nuggetty, friendly and talkative little boy, but he had a splash of Old Nick in him. If he wasn't allowed to do a thing, he'd go frantic needing to do it. If the clothes-washing water was so hot that Mam had to use a stick to stir it, Caffy's sole purpose in living became the dipping of his fingers into it. If there was something breakable sitting on the table, Caffy would find the means to crack it over his head. Already that morning he had caught his curls in the wringer and scalped bald a patch the size of a penny. "He's doing my head in with his pestering; take him off with yourself and Audrey," said Mam, and it was me who heaved a sigh. I knew that, as soon as we were clear of the house, Audrey would send me packing with the baby under tow.

It happened as I predicted, so I was ready to refuse. Caffy was swinging from the crook of Audrey's elbow and I said, "He wants to stay with you."

"Harper!" she whined. Izzy was lurking in the distance, inspecting some lump in the ground—he didn't like to get involved in these wranglings. "Harper, please, just do as I say!"

"You'll go away and leave me dragging him around all day."

"We won't go away, I promise. When Izzy and I finish talking, I'll call you and you can come back. Then I'll watch Caffy for the rest of the day."

I didn't believe her, and shook my head stubbornly. Audrey gave a strangled cry. She bent, and wrenched my ear close to her. "Harper," she breathed, "this will be the last time. If you go away today, I'll never ask you to go away again. I mean it, I promise. But it's important you go away today."

"Why?"

"Because Izzy might ask me to marry him today. I think he's going to."

I narrowed my eyes. She had been saying something similar for almost a year and I was beginning to suspect that either Izzy had never heard of the idea of marriage or that he didn't like Audrey as much as she supposed. I was hardened to her fancy now and could be, in the face of it, as obstinate as a mule. And yet, I had never abandoned all hope, just as Audrey herself had not. I had a conviction that if there ever were a wedding, there would be something in it for me.

Regardless, my bribery price was high. "Will you give me your hair clip?"

"But I only have one!"

"I only want one."

She showed her teeth and hesitated. I waited. "All right," she hissed.

I took Caffy's hand and pulled him away from her; he squawked and shouted but couldn't wrestle himself free. I dragged him thrashing through the grass while smugly contemplating my new prize. I had long coveted the hair clip but if things went on like this much longer, Audrey would own nothing more to give me. That would be a sorry day, and one rather quickly coming, but I was loath to lower my fee. I put this quandary from my mind and turned my energy to my task.

It was important, when Audrey sent me off, to stay beyond sight of Mam and Da, for a spy is not meant to lose her quarry. I coaxed Caffy along, murmuring so he had to pipe down to hear me, keeping a sharp eye on the house. Da was safely out in the paddock but Mam would soon step into the yard to hang out the washing. I did a broad half loop and settled in the dust behind the animal shelter, where we couldn't be seen from the clothesline. From here I could see the rear of the house, glimmering away. Caffy could see it too and wanted to go home, so I twitched a stalk in his face until he was distracted and laughing. "Want to play a game?" I asked.

"What game?"

"You hide, and I'll hunt for you."

"Don't look, and count."

I turned my head to the shelter and began to count. There wasn't anywhere challenging he could hide, what with just the long patchy grass around and some weedy eucalypts in the distance, but Caffy was too young to know that, being just three and a half. I peeked past the shelter and studied the house, watching for sign of Mam. Away in the paddock I could see Devon riding Champion. They were cantering in circles. I droned through the numbers, wondered if Izzy had finally asked the question. It surely wouldn't take long to say the words. Marry me. Oh, would you marry me? Will you marry me, Audrey, and let Harper live with us so I might see her every day?

Devon was yelling now, and pointing at the ground. He was yelling there was a snake, and I huddled nervously. Snakes gave me the shudders. Mam always said, "Just leave them; they'll go their way," but Da was more for hacking off their heads. He was bound to come running any moment, shovel in hand for the deed. Suddenly and to my horror I saw Mam, ducking through the fence and calling to Devon to quit his raucous bellowing and leave the poor snake be. I scanned about and couldn't see Izzy and Audrey. If they were out of sight, so must I be. I glanced over my shoulder and Caffy, too, was out of sight. Da had arrived at the snake now, and he and Mam were staring down intently. I chewed my nails, jittery. I was pinned here, behind the shed, for as long as Mam and Da were standing where they would see any move I made. Caffy, being three and a half, had not an ounce of patience, and if I didn't come searching for him soon he would get bored and peevish, and that would spell disaster.

"Caffy?" I whispered. "Where are you?"

He thought I was trying to trick him, I reckoned, and didn't answer me. I squirmed about uncomfortably, my legs dimpled by sticks and stones. I wished Da would get on with the hacking. I could hear Mam distantly, arguing over the reptile's fate. The sun grew suddenly hotter, you could feel it like a scald on your skin. I eased backward to where the shelter's shadow lay, taking the weight from my smarting knees. I heard a faint groaning and knew Caffy was getting irritable. "Hush," I crooned, "hush, hush." Finally, the thunk. I looked and Mam was marching to the house, swishing her skirts angrily. Da held high the decapitated snake and it was spilling blood into the ground. Caffy moaned miserably and I scurried forward on all fours. "Here I come," I warned him. "I'm coming to find you, Caffy."

The grass spiked me in the rib cage as I scanned for his chubby face. He wouldn't have gone far and the noise he made had sounded close; between the shelter and the weedy trees was only a spread of balding silver grass with no rocks or hollows that might hide him. He was wearing dusk-blue overalls and curled up in the grass he should have been easy to see, yet I was having difficulty. "Caffy?" I queried, and propped upon my haunches. I was careful not to sound cross or worried, which would simply encourage him. I shaded my eyes, baffled.

I looked at the trees but he was only little, he couldn't get up there.

"Caffy!" I said, louder. "Mamma wants you to come home."

Then I heard him, and whirled. He should have been behind me, but he wasn't. I waved my hands lest I wasn't seeing something and my fingers cut through empty air. I heard a gurgle and it came from my feet, making me spring sideways with a squeak of alarm, but it was just grass there. For a second I was going mad, I thought he must have shrunk to the size of a gnat and was perched on a blade. I dipped a hand in the grass and my hand kept dipping until my arm had disappeared into the earth. I slashed aside the grass and stared, aghast. In the ground before me was one of the holes dug by the well-sinker. After all this time it gaped still, its ragged black mouth snarling open. It was dry inside, but it was deep and narrow. Caffy had fallen down it.

I staggered, I swear. I almost hit the dirt. I reached my arm into the depths and grappled for him desperately, knocking loose clods of hard, ochre dirt that dropped into the darkness. I couldn't reach him and stood, reeling queasily. Mam would have a conniption about this, and I bit my lip against a burning threat of tears. If I could manage to get him out, I might never have to tell her. I darted into the shelter and searched for a rope, finding only the lead clipped to Champion's halter. It was short, shorter than me, but it was better than nothing. Outside, I put my face to the mouth of the well and called, "Hold on to Champy's halter, Caffy, so I can pull you out."

I dribbled the halter down the well and kept dribbling it, its buckles clinking against the walls. When I was holding hardly any rope I gave it a tug and the halter flung up lightly into my hands. I chirped distraughtly and fed it down again, wailing, "Get hold of the halter, Caffy!"

But he didn't get hold. I thought he must be playing. Then it came to me that maybe he couldn't get hold, even if he wanted, because the halter didn't reach him. Gagging, I threw the rope aside and plunged my head in the hole, crashing my ribs against the earth and shearing skin from my chin. I couldn't see him but I could hear him mewling and I knew how he looked when he grizzled that way. His hands would be tugging at his lips, there'd be water pooling in his eyes. The well stank and was airless and I had to wrench, spluttering, away. "Caffy!" I barked, as if shouting would wake me up from this, or stop him teasing me. It simply made him cry, and in anguish I began clawing the dirt.

The dirt was hard. Not a drop of rain had fallen for months. The grass was needle sharp and leathery, its wiry roots meshed with jagged stones; the hot red earth was cracked and compacted and grazed bloody the tips of my fingers. Bull-ants ran in frantic circles and flies dithered before my sweating face; the heat was pressing me to the ground and sapping away my strength. A grass seed drove beneath my nail and then I was rocking on my rump, coddling the pain and whimpering. Mam was going to murder me and all my trying was useless, just as it had been when Tin was smothered in the mud.

Tin: the thought of him leaped on me, making me leap, and I was charging, howling, for home. My bawling summoned everyone, including Izzy and Audrey. I remember Mam rushing alongside me and the ripping sound of the grass catching at her hem, her blue eyes wide with fearfulness and growing wider as she ran closer to the thing that made her afraid. She cried, "Why weren't you watching him, Audrey?"

But if Audrey had an answer Mam would not have stopped to hear it and by then everything was confusion. Da had his shovel and there was a splash of blood on it that had stained the wooden handle. He slammed the blade into the mouth of the hole and the ground fissured, loosing into the well a cascade of clods and stones. "Stop!" yelped Mam. "You'll close it in on top of him!"

Caffy, hearing voices, intensified his wails. Izzy and Devon had thrown themselves on their bellies and were gouging the well's maw. "Da," I said, "get Tin—"

A lump of dirt sloughed off the hole and plunged into the blackness, Mam and Audrey screeching to see it go. Audrey did not stop screeching; she sank to the ground with her arms around her waist and shrieked into the earth. I spun and sprinted. Please, Baby Jesus, I prayed, please make him near.

I ran to the mouth of the newest tunnel, the one that slunk around the house, and shouted into it. Glancing back I saw my family clustered at the well, saw Devon on Champion galloping in the direction of the road. I ducked my head and roared out Tin's name. I couldn't see anything in the tunnel, it was as pitch as night when your eyes are closed. "Tin!" I roared, my voice streaming along a passage I just had to trust was there. I flopped to my stomach, limp with exhaustion and frustration and despair. Why was he never around when I needed him, I wondered bitterly. I seemed to need him all the time, and he was never there.

"Harper! Come here!"

I sprang up and raced to where Da was standing with the halter and the lead rope swinging in his hands. I smelled old booze on him. "Chicken," he said, "be a brave girl. We'll tie the rope to your ankles and you can go down and grab him—"

"No!" Mam yanked me away. "You're not putting another of them underground!"

Da grabbed my wrist and pulled me forward. "She has to do it! We have to try!"

"No, I said!"

"You want him to die? Do you?"

"I want them all to live, you fool!"

"Stop it!" Audrey sobbed, clutching at her hair. "Let Harper go!"

They each released their hold on my wrists, and my arms dropped to my sides. Sweat was flooding down Da's crimson face, while Mam's was as white as a cloud. Caffy was crying, not strongly or loudly.

"I don't fit down the well," I mumbled, softly and ashamed. "I already tried."

Mam spun away from us, her hands fluttering to

her eyes. She didn't come close to the well, after that—instead, each step she took carried her farther from it, until she hardly seemed there at all. Ghosting, she became ghostly; when I reached for her, she could not take my hand because she was no longer able to touch. "Mam," I pleaded, "Mam—"

Tin stepped from behind her, his gaze taking everything in. Caffy went quiet and Audrey lifted her head and in the silence Tin came to crouch beside me, his wrists resting on the flank of the hole. He bent his elbows until his shoulder blades jutted like wings and his nose hovered above the well and he sniffed, as if gauging the mood of the ground. He put an ear to the earth and closed his eyes, listening to the dirt's soundless tune. He sat up and we watched as he crumbled a clod between his hands and passed his gritty fingers across his lips and chin. Then he got to his feet and walked backward, carefully, as though he were treading a wire, stopping when he was a dozen or more paces distant from both us and the well. He marked the earth where he stood with the scrape of a toe. Without a word, without looking at us or saying how we might help him, he shrugged off his rabbit rags and, naked, he started to dig.

You could see what Da had seen so early, how he had the digging gift. His hands, they flew, and you didn't see them as ten separate fingers but rather as two curving claws which left rents in the density of the packed solid earth. Izzy was staring with his mouth lazing open, never having seen Tin but having heard as much as anyone knew—heard of the hair that had lost its curl and chestnut color and now hung scraggy down his spine and no shade you could accurately describe; heard of the eyes stained with only a faint wash of the deep blue they had been, larger and rounder than you would expect them and ringed with thick, protecting lashes; heard of the ears whose tips folded over like a dog's can, to keep the mechanisms clear. He'd heard, too, of Tin's neat smallness, of how he grew slowly and looked older than his eight years, of his skin being translucent and somehow looser than it should be, so he could twist about freely within it, and how it was glazed, almost waxy, for warding out the damp. Izzy had heard this, but never seen it before. We had seen him, but we had never seen him like this. The old mystery was solved, that day, regarding what happened to the dirt Tin threw from his diggings, which we had never been able to find. The answer was that there was no dirt, or none worth speaking of. The earth simply fell away beneath his hands, like water parts for a swimmer. It was as if the ground adored Tin's attentions and, as a dog will shift its legs to better allow a belly scratch or a cat will bob upward to meet a petting hand, the earth eased his way by offering no obstacle and did what it could to encourage him. I held my breath to watch him, understanding for the first time that Tin was not simply a boy who lived underground: he was loved and wanted under there, and irresistibly summoned.

But nonetheless his digging took time, as though the earth were willing but doltish and in need of tolerant guiding. He never glanced up from his work, not when Mr. Godwin and Mr. Murphy arrived and stood about with brows knit helplessly, not when Audrey sang down the well for Caffy, not when Caffy's noise became weak and broken, not when Mam sat in the grass and cried. He was digging at an angle, knowing exactly where Caffy hung and meaning to meet him at a junction. Mr. Godwin murmured, "Surely it would make faster digging if he went straight down."

"Let him do as he thinks fit. If anyone knows about excavation, it's him."

"Aye."

"Caffy? Tin will get you. He's making his way to you. Good lad, Caffy."

Tin was beyond sight now, burrowed in the earth. Sometimes a dog would disappear after him and emerge to shake off sandy clouds. Cicadas started calling suddenly and I could feel my skin beginning to burn. Caffy was groaning feebly, and not all the time. He'd been trapped down the hole for more than an hour.

"How much longer, do you reckon?'

"I don't know. I know nothing about this. A child isn't stuck in a well every day."

"You still there? Caffy?"

"Do you hear us, Caffy?"

"Caffy boy? Caffy?"

Caffy. Audrey was slumped beside Mam but not touching her. I crawled to my sister and she put her arms round me. My face was scarlet, sunburned to the bone; her face was gray, pale and dulled as a winter sky. Other neighbors arrived, stared down the well despondently, stood with their shovels idly by. Mrs. Murphy gathered up Mam and coaxed her inside the house. The cows watched from the shade of the shelter, turning their jaws pensively. Godwin's lean greyhounds lay about, chiseled rib cages heaving, insects twinged from delicate ears.

"Jesus."

A heft of earth had split from the side of the hole and plummeted.

"Maybe it never found him."

"Caffy?"

He didn't answer, but he'd been quiet for a time.

"That hole should have been filled right after it was dug," I heard Harry Robertson say low. "Flute's become a careless man."

Bernie Osborne sucked his yellow cigarette. "He's keeping his head for the moment, though."

"Not like that business with the shanty. He was a sorry sight then. Needed a good shaking."

"He's not the man he once was, even now. Hard to talk to, and the like."

"Maybe he can't sink any lower than he is and that's what's holding him upright."

Robertson smiled wryly, and they both turned away when they saw me standing there.

Unexpectedly Tin stepped out of the ground, smearing his face on his forearm. Over his elbow he looked at us, the useless crowd. He shook his hair and flexed his fingers. He had a torn knee which was weeping a colorless fluid. If he had wanted something, a drink or water for rinsing his eyes, he changed his mind and went without. If he'd had something to say, he chose to say nothing. He went back down. "Lawd," whispered someone. Over two hours had passed.

"Caffy's probably sleeping down there. Probably asleep."

"Aye, he's sleeping, that's what he's doing. He'll be awake all night, having slept the day away."

"Tin'll find him all cozy as a kitten, laughing at his dreams."

" . . . Bless him. God bless his little soul."

I was dozing when Tin brought him out, my head on Audrey's thigh. I opened my eyes and blinked at the glaring whiteness of the sky. For a moment I was in a colorless and noiseless world. I rolled over and saw the silver grass, the gray shirts of the neighbors, the blackness of a sniffing dog, the olive of the eucalypt leaves. Tin was standing, wanly luminous, cradling a dusk-blue bundle. Still there was no noise.

Tin bowed his head and his hair fanned over Caffy. He smoothed down Caffy's fair curls. Then he looked at us, his eyes flitting anxiously—I knew he was searching for Mam. Not seeing her, he came to Audrey. She stood and took the child from him. Tin, his arms empty, stepped away. Audrey's hand fluttered on Caffy's cheek. "He died," she said.

Everyone drifted toward the house, following Audrey in a sorrowful procession. They didn't stay to see Tin fold into the grass, shivering with exhaustion. His hands were battered and swollen and he held them away from his body; the ochre earth had stained and spattered him. I hesitated, my heart telling me to stay with him but my head not understanding why he should need comforting — he had hardly known Caffy, after all.

"Tin," I said, "I know that you tried. I know you dug the best you could."

Such defeat and anguish came into his face that my heart lurched and cleanly broke. I lingered there with nothing else to say, my throat and eyes parched arid, sharp-edged insects whipping by me through the white hot windless day.

My mother and father had held up the sky, the sun, the stars and the moon, but they didn't anymore. The shanty had fallen and Da was different; I still loved him, but he wasn't the Da from before. When you told him something, you couldn't be sure he was listening. If you thought a thing was important, he might curse or smile and say it wasn't really. He had stopped snaring rabbits when the pelts became wastage and had taken instead to shooting them, although we only had two boxes of shot and no money to buy more and although it meant picking black pellets from the stew, and the hours he had once spent scraping rabbit skins were spent wandering the district with a twig and a dog and the cows and his flask, a moth-eaten troupe lacklusterly seeking fodder. At home he would leave the rifle by the door, on a tilt like a kipping soldier. There was something about the rifle that always reminded me of Da, its ashy color and thinness, the burden of its own weight. Devon quit school and took up doing most of Da's old chores, as if Da were incapable or dead weary. Sometimes, as Da had done, Devon took a thing to town to pawn. He pawned the box that Grandda's money had come in and brought home secondhand shoes for me.

Mam became a ghost at the mouth of the well and she stayed that way a long time. In evenings on the veranda she talked of how things had been when she was a girl, stories I had never heard before. When she told these stories, her eyes shone. She would dab at them with the corner of her apron, laughing while she cried. Through the heat of the day she moved like a wind-up toy, bustling with energy when the key was turned tight, gradually going slow and teetering and finally coming to a halt, emptiness ringing around her, staring ahead at nothing, forgetting what she meant to say. She might be doing something, something usual like stirring or pegging the clothes, and she would stop. She would walk off and disappear for hours, wandering the creek bed, the scrub and the hills. I would run about searching for her, calling out her name. Inside myself I knew she was safe, and that she would return, but I could not help it, anyway; in the months after Caffy's death, I couldn't bear losing sight of her. Audrey would bring me home, talking to me, holding on to my hand. She and I never spoke about Caffy, not even when there was no one around to hear. I had wanted to—I longed to explain that my intentions had been good, how I'd hoped so much for only good things to happen; I craved to speak of the sooty cloud that overhung me now, and how nothing would ever be good anymore—but I stopped trying when I saw that talking about him might make a wind-up toy out of Audrey, too. Her eyes would go hooded and I would feel her perishing inside. So I covered my mouth and buried my brother, for fear of losing a sister. I needed someone to care for me in the melancholy months that dragged behind that breezeless morning, and I understood that my mother and father were gone: Audrey and Devon had become all I had. Tin was digging as if the digging he'd done in the past was practice or pretend. We'd hear that he had been seen many miles off and, seen, had vanished into thin air. Only, there was no thin air in Tin's world; if he vanished, it was into the opposite of air. If he could do that, so far from home, his web of tunnels must have become a kingdom and it would be futile to search for him. So, for me, it was Devon and Audrey, Audrey and Devon, and Izzy, too, who visited most days and never spoke of Caffy, either, but had been feverish for days after and fragile for a month, and I clung to the three of them. When it was winter and cold and I was hungry, it was Audrey I grieved to, not my Mam; it was Devon, not Da, who cracked my knuckles smartly for making the complaint. I fretted that a calamity would befall one or all of them and became a hectoring bore, badgering to know what they were doing and where they were going and how long they would be away. In private I composed chants and spells that I cast to keep them safe. By day my concern was loud and smothering; at night I would lie clutching my pillow, soundlessly praying that they would not leave me and go where Mam and Da had gone.

So when Vandery Cable arrived with his proposition, my heart was almost drowned by my terror. He stood at the door like the Reaper, saying, "It will ease the situation here."

"Mr. Cable," Devon said flatly, not rising from his chair, "I'm surprised you haven't had it to the teeth, being decent to this family."

Cable smiled grimly, brushing the insult aside. He had a purpose and kept his mind to it. "It would benefit both parties. I need a housekeeper, the occasional meal prepared. I'm told Miss Flute's learned cooking from Rose Murphy."

Audrey was standing at the fireplace, the ladle drooping in her hand. In the cooking pot burbled a stew of rabbit and water. Cable couldn't see into the pot from where he stood on the threshold. If I'd been quicker-thinking, I would have beckoned him over and made him look. "I was taught by Mam, mostly," she said.

He ignored that, too. "I pay wages on the last Friday of every month. The money would be yours, to do with as you choose, but if some of it were to find its way into this house, I don't suppose that would be a bad thing."

Audrey glanced across the room. Da was grasping the arms of his chair, straining forward like a hound on a chain. Mam's hand had moved closer to Devon, as though touching him was sanctuary. Audrey asked, "May I have a few days to decide, Mr. Cable?"

"I hope you'll consider it seriously, Miss Flute."

"I will. But I'm needed here, you see—"

"You could do a lot of good, with the money you would earn."

She fumbled over her answer: "Thank you," she said senselessly.

He gave her a final piercing stare before propping his hat on his head. "Good night, then," he said.

As soon as the door was closed Devon growled, "No. Tell him no. That man's a dog."

"Devon." Mam took her gaze from the table. "He only wants to help."

"Does he? Why? Why does he always want to help? What does he get out of it?"

"Devvy—"

"No—think about it! He's not a charity, he'll want his pound of flesh one day. Or maybe he'll just work Audrey a week and send her home with nothing to show."

"Now, Devon," muttered Da, and Devon, though outraged, subsided, because no one wanted Cable's escaped sows to come charging into the room.

"He gave us the barn. Without it, we wouldn't have the house. He's given us some wise advice."

"Like selling Tin to the circus?" I was hunched in

a corner bristling, baring my teeth like a rat.

"Hush, Harper."

"But he said our cows were useless, Da—"

"And he hasn't found that bull he promised."

"He didn't promise anything, Devon. He only said he'd try."

"I think he is a decent man," Mam said, "although he struggles to show it."

"The money, too," said Da artlessly.

Audrey lifted her eyes to them, but they were nodding at the floor. "Yes," she said, "the money. I should tell him that I'll do it."

"Audrey!" I squealed, springing up afrizz. "You can't!"

"Do whatever you think best," said Da. "A house-keeper who knows her job is never lost for employment."

"If she wants to be someone's servant all her life," snapped Devon, but Da serenely did not hear. "If you felt inclined to give us a small amount each week, we might soon have enough to put in a crop or buy a bull of our own. Of course, we wouldn't expect it."

Devon looked deadly at him. "Jesus," he hissed.

Later, when it was dark and the house was silent, I crept on my knees to her bedside. "Audrey," I whispered, "don't go to Mr. Cable's. I don't like him."

In the starlight slanting past the shutter I could see her eyes glittering and her fingers fiddled distractedly with the nightdress ribbon at her throat. "I don't like him, either. But he's not asking us to like him, Harper."

I clamped my hands beneath me, wrestling for the words. "Audrey, who will look out for me, if you go to Mr. Cable's?"

She smiled. "You're eleven years old. You don't need anyone looking out for you."

"But I feel as if I do."

"Devon will be here."

"It wouldn't be the same."

"Mam will take care of you."

I sagged and said nothing, heart-heavy. Her eyes left me and went to the window.

"I want to go," she sighed. "I want to go somewhere Caffy wasn't."

My blood fluttered. "Do you think about him?"

"Don't you?"

"I do." I shuffled closer on my knees. "I wasn't watching. I wasn't watching him, when he went down the well. But I thought he would be safe. I didn't think anything bad could happen to him."

"It's not your fault." She turned on her side and frowned at me. "Never think it was your fault, Harper. It was me—I'm to blame. Blame me, all right? I should have been holding his hand. I would give everything, if I could hold it now."

"But you had to talk to Izzy, remember? He was going to ask to marry you."

Audrey's fingers twitched on the pillow. "Do you know what we talked about, after you and Caffy went off that day? Clouds. He kept talking about clouds. I was thinking, Why's he telling me this airy-fairy? Who cares about clouds? It seemed mad, to me—I was wondering if he'd gone mad. And then I heard you yelling that Caffy had fallen down the well. I thought you were wrong because Caffy was right there, with me, and then I remembered he wasn't. For a moment everything was strange. And then it was awful, and it hasn't stopped being that way. Sometimes I can hardly breathe; I can't fill my lungs. I can hear him crying and he won't go quiet—but maybe he will, if I go to Mr. Cable's. Maybe I won't be able to hear him, if I go a long way from here."

"But what about me?" I slid my hand into hers and squeezed desperately. "I was watching Da kill a snake. Caffy was whimpering and I was ignoring him, I didn't help him, and now I can't ever help him, but I still remember his whimpering. So maybe I can come with you, if you go to Mr. Cable's?"

"Harper . . ."

"Please, Audrey! I don't want to stay here by myself. Caffy isn't here and Mam—she isn't here—and I'll be alone, if you go too."

She held my hand and looked a long time into my face. Then, "Go to bed," she told me. "Don't worry."

I crawled away miserably and slept a wakeful, troubled night. But the next day, when Devon came in for lunch with cattle spikes shedding off him, Audrey set the soup on the table and said, "I'm not going to work for Mr. Cable. Mam. Da."

"Now, Audrey—"

"It's decided, Da."

"We could use the money. And I feel we owe Mr. Cable."

"Owe him what? *What*?"

Audrey disregarded Devon. "I'm needed here. At least, for now."

"Let her do as she thinks best, Court."

I was grinning and couldn't grin more fiercely when Mam said that, although I would have liked to. It was the sort of thing she might have said in the time before the shanty fell. It was like feeling the sun rub your nose after winter.

"Good," said Devon. "I'll go over and tell him this afternoon."

Da was sullen, saying nothing while Audrey filled his bowl. Rabbit in water is harsh on the nose and eye, and Audrey chuckled as she scooped. "I don't know where he got the idea I can cook," she laughed.

"You're doing your best with what you have."

"You are, Audrey."

I was gazing at her adoringly and she tucked back my hair. "Aren't you tired of rabbit, Harper?"

"Yes, but I don't mind."

Mam considered us—Devon, then Audrey, then me. I fidgeted under her inspection, chewing my lip and bringing my bowl closer, and the steam of the soup dampened my cheeks. Mam turned unexpectedly to Da. "Court," she said, "I know you're fond of the cows but it's time, now. The children will become ill if they don't get something decent into them. If you can't do it, Art Campbell said he would."

Da's fist was bloodless around his spoon. "I'm telling you, Thora, it'd be doing a foolish thing. Things will get better and when they do, you'll see that I'm right. You've no vision for the future, that's the problem."

"Vandery Cable said to save them for a day such as this. Not for a future day—for this day."

Da ground his teeth. He glared at us and the room was soundless but for the thwack of a blowfly striking the ceiling. "Only one, Court," Mam said gently. "You can keep the other two."

"All right!" he shouted, making us jump. "All right. Don't blame me later, is all I ask. Don't blame me, when things are not so bad."

We did not smile or say anything. That afternoon Devon rode over to Cable's, but Da did not kill a cow. We waited, saying nothing, but he didn't do it the next day or the next. So I pushed away my plate of rabbit and water, hoping that would make him hurry.

I pushed away my plate and slouched. Everyone saw me do it but even Devon glanced aside. I sat with my eyes down, hardly daring to breathe. Afterward, when I was clearing the table, Audrey said, "Scrape your plate out for the animals."

Outside the dogs crowded me, their whiskery faces eager and struggling to keep themselves civilized. They knew that arguing with one another meant losing food to somedog else and they stood like statues drooling while I emptied soup into their bowls; if any of them heard the knock at the door, none of them were about to waste time investigating. I went back inside to find two vinegar-faced traveling salesmen skulking by the wall. They had shoelaces and matches they were hawking. "Harper," said Mam, "do you need laces?"

I shook my head dourly, keeping my eye on the

travelers, edging my way nearer to Devon. All the men who came to our door were thin and tousled, some more gone to seed than others. Some had no dignity and would sniffle on seeing a family, bemoaning their long-lost own. Some joked and played tricks with cards and coins and I liked those ones the best. The pair standing bow-spined in the kitchen were young and pungent, their suits wafting mildew. The elder had a rash flaming between his chin and coat collar; the younger one's eyes rolled like oily marbles toward Audrey. They did not seem surprised when Mam told them she couldn't buy, and the elder scratched his rash blandly. "We can give you a cup of tea," said Mam, pitying them.

"Or port," offered Da. "We've a drop of that to spare."

"Tea will be dandy," said the elder, and they sat, all shins and elbows, when Da drew out the chairs. "Stretch to remember when last I had a sip of tea. Not since I left home, I reckon."

"Are you up from the city?"

"Are, missus. Left the mother and sisters behind. The mother didn't want us to go but we heard things weren't so crook away from the city. Finding, of course, there's plenty who heard the same and now here's as crook as anywhere. Roads out here, you're wading through down-and-outs. It's right, though, that the brother and I make our own way. The mother and the sisters will do better without two extra stomachs to feed."

"There's stomachs in this house," spoke Da, "that choose to go hungry. Rabbit isn't good enough for them."

I scuttled sideways to where Audrey had filled the washing trough, and took up the sponge. "You're brothers, then?" asked Mam.

"Brothers, missus. Himself's Christopher, I'm Ben."

I dipped a plate gingerly, holding it in my fingertips. The water was boiling and my face crunched at the prospect of being scorched—and caught the younger, Christopher, smirking at the sight. He and his brother were flat-faced scarecrows, their black hair cropped to a prickle on their scalps, their suits stiffened instead of softened with age. I turned my back on his vile leering. Devon asked, "What's it like, then, in the city?"

"Fearful. Mind you, there's some you'll see who aren't feeling it at all. They're the ones who say there's work going everywhere for decent folk who aren't lazy. Not true, though. There's plenty of decent folk where we come from, and it's fearful there."

"Fearful how?"

The elder took his tea without slurping and leaned back in his chair. "Tell you what fearful is. Fearful is losing the job you've been doing since you left school at fourteen and walking the streets in search of employment, lining up with hundreds when a single vacancy comes up on a factory floor. Fearful's coming home to hungry children, sending them off to soup kitchens for a bit of jam and a spud. Fearful is being tipped from your home because you can't pay the rent. The family's on the street then, sleeping in the gutter or holed-up in a flour-sack tent. Some well-to-do complains you're an eyesore and the authorities burn your tent and move the lot of you on. Having your existence sapped away by constant want and woe, looking at your littlies and knowing the future holds nothing for them, losing all the respect and worthiness you ever had because something happened that had nothing to do with you—that's what fearful is, in my opinion."

The younger one put in, as if it were the most pleasing thing, "They're burning the fences. Say that."

171

"Hmph. People burn fences to stay warm."

"No fences." The younger nodded eerily. His brother took no notice but clawed absently at his rash.

"There's the welfare though, isn't there?"

"The sustenance, if you can get it. They're picky about who does—they might give it you once and never again, or maybe never at all. There's ladies who decide if you're desperate enough. If you ain't desperate to their satisfaction, you get diddly. If your clothes are dirty or your floor needs mopping or the littlies are crawling with nits, you won't be getting a penny. You're not trying hard enough to stay decent, decide these ladies, so you're not worthy of helping. Rumor is, though, that if you're a friend of these ladies, the sustenance comes nice and regular."

"But that's ridiculous," said Devon. The elder nodded with weary knowingness.

"Whole world's gone ridiculous, I say. There's stealing, there's looting, there's jealousies turning neighbor against neighbor. People wear rags now. Newborns get left on doorsteps. Men stand outside pubs just to sniff the air—it's as close as they can get to swallowing what's inside."

"Won't you have some port, then?" said Da, reaching for the bottle.

"No sir, thank you, the tea does us fine. The mother always told us, stay away from the plonk. Get a taste for that and ruin is not far away. Are you planning on going to the city, lad?"

All of us looked alarmed at Devon, who shrugged. "Just asking."

"Stay here. Where we come from, there's gangs of boys like yourself passing their lives on street corners, nothing to do with themselves, watching their youth fritter away. They stand about, chatting up the girls, spooking the passersby. They're bored and that brings out the bad elements among them, the theft and the gambling, but most of them are just harmless lads. The police knock them around regardless, arrest them for nothing, so they hate the police. Hate each other, too, and there's fighting on the streets, the chains, the knives . . ." He trailed off, staring into his cup morosely and shaking his bristly head. "No, that's no life for a young man. It's why I was determined to bring himself out here with me. I won't have him going the way of the larrikin."

It looked like the rescue had come too late, to

me. Christopher sat like a razor bent to fit the chair, tense as some ill-fed fighting dog. His gaze zipped like a fly across the room, alighting on Audrey and skittering off again. "Say about the ladies," he croaked.

"Himself wants me to tell you about the ladies. Things are different for them. Some have jobs because it's cheaper to employ a female, you know? In factories and the like. Find many a young lady supporting her whole family—mother, father, the smaller ones. Proud and happy to be doing so, too. The oldest sister is that way, sews petticoats, admirable. Hurts her neck bending over the machine but she's fortunate compared to some. What some must do is a tragedy, and a fate I wouldn't wish on any respectable female."

"What do you mean?"

"Hush, Harper."

The salesman nodded deeply, which made his rash flare. "Better she doesn't understand. Things are fearful, like I say. But I'll tell you what I think's the worst thing, and it's to do with the ladies. Some of them, the only way they can hold their heads high when they've got nothing, no money, no milk for the baby, no husband worth having— the only way they can show the neighbors that they're still respectable people is to keep the house clean. The idea being, I suppose, that decent folk live in decent homes. And there's women going demented trying to make the house spotless, women who start to see dirt everywhere, as if it's got in under their eyes, women going slowly mad. The lucky ones get sent to hospital but most of them aren't lucky. Most of them die jabbering on the kitchen floor, killing themselves to show they're upstanding. Dying for dirt in a dirty old world. It's funny, in a way: something went askew on the other side of the globe and now our mothers are losing their minds."

The terrible Christopher gave a giggle. His brother darted a glance at him. "We should go," he decided suddenly. "We're bringing sorrow into your home."

"There's more tea in the pot . . ."

"Thank you, no. We mustn't get too settled, not with the road awaiting us. You've got a nice setup, here. Fine house, and no doubt the odd animal or two?"

"We have three Red Poll heifers," said Da, stately. "People don't keep beef around here and they said I was a fool to have bought them—some of the doubters were sadly close to home. They reckoned you couldn't keep cattle fed and healthy, not on this poor ground. I've done it, though, done it going on three years. It's not easy, no: I've walked them ten miles, some days, for a mouthful of grass. It's been a struggle, but they're alive, and they're thriving, and I reckon I might have started building up the herd soon, had not other people had other ideas. Sometimes you wonder why you bother doing anything, wasting your hopes and energies."

"Is that right?" said the salesman. "Is that right."

"We also have two chickens," added Da.

"Well, sir, you would be envied, where we come from. You're lucky people, and deserving to be. Christopher and myself thank you for the hospitality. Long life and God's blessings to you."

They gathered their matches and laces and, with lingering glances and mauling of throat, went out into the evening, leaving behind a cloud of staleness. I remember thinking how strange it was, that man calling us lucky. Had Caffy left no mark on us? What about our drifting Da, and our ghostly Mam? Or was it that some marks showed clearly but we were lucky anyway, because there was worse that could have happened? I went to bed with my empty stomach grumbling, feeling childish to have ever complained, but nonetheless insulted. We had had, I felt, misfortune to match the best of them.

In the morning, the heifers and chickens were gone. You could see where the cows had been shepherded through a stretch of fence where the rails had been taken down. The chickens had been plucked from their roost as casual as apples from a tree. On the ground was a drift of harplike feathers where their necks had been wrung. No one said it and there was never any proof but we knew, we simply knew that those two city boys had done it, that dainty-sipping older one and his half-baked younger brother. Devon saddled Champion and galloped around the district for days, asking if anyone had sighted a pair of scarecrows driving three mottled cows in front and a hen slung over a shoulder. Such a band should have been easy to track but this one never was: the salesmen had taken our animals and just melted into the ground.

When Devon came home on the fourth day of searching, he unbuckled the horse's saddle and dumped it on the ground before flopping on the veranda and staring silently at the orange sky. All of us looked at him without speaking. We could hear finches chattering in the tussocks and the steady blowing of Champion.

"Well, you tried, Devvy."

He didn't answer, kept his eyes on the sky. Audrey returned to combing my hair.

"The dogs," said Da. "They could have barked. We might have woken up if they had barked. Useless. I should shoot the lot of them, and serve them right."

"Leave them be," Mam told him dully. "Leave the dogs alone, Court. They've got the same as we have, now. Nothing but their beating hearts."

In the months that followed I used to ponder, now and then, over what the travelers had said about fearfulness and misery and how those things were entwined with money somehow, as if money is a seed that sprouts poison. I remembered the time when Da had trapped rabbits and sold the faultless pelts to the dealer and I wondered at how happy we must have been then, how rich we were made by the shillings he brought home. But sense told me shillings could not have made us wealthy, and I understood that we had always been poor. How young I must have been then, to have been happy anyway.

I ate the soup that was put before me now. Devon was snaring the rabbits that went into it, to save on the shot. But the shot went missing, any-way: Da pawned it, leaving only what was loaded in the rifle. He bought whisky with the money and I told Audrey, "You should pour it on the ground."

"Why?" Her voice was calm—she never both-ered getting angry anymore.

"It would serve him right."

"Pouring the whisky away won't bring the shot back."

But me, I was angry all the time.

Snaring never stopped as many as shooting did, regardless of whether you were chasing the pelts or the meat. We were always hungry, and Da caught a rasping cold. That winter I walked the surrounds inquiring after odd jobs to do and sometimes I'd be given a coin for stacking wood or plucking and giz-zarding a chicken. These were things people could do themselves for nothing and finally Audrey com-manded me to stay home, saying I was earning off compassion. Rose Murphy came around one day and asked why she hadn't seen me flogging my tal-ents at the door. I told her what Audrey had told me: "I was causing grief. I was making others share our trouble."

She gazed at me for a time, sitting beside me on the veranda. My hair was raggle-taggle over my face and I kept my eyes lowered behind it. I glanced up when I felt her turn away, knowing my cheeks were burning red. She was staring at the trampled yard, at the pale clothes on the line, at the bony pile of dogs. "It doesn't seem so long ago," she sighed, "when that baby was born and I smacked you for your sass. I don't suppose you remember it, you were only the youngest thing."

"I remember," I said, leaning close to the warmth of her, hugging up my knees. "I remember Caffy being small enough to sleep in the dresser drawer. I remember Tin before he went underground, how he used to follow Mam like a puppy. I remember Devon and me playing handball in the yard and Audrey wanting to play but she was no good, the ball kept hitting her head. I remember Da breathing fire and Mam getting cross but hiding her face so we wouldn't see her laughing. I remember when we had the shanty but we didn't have the fence or the well or the cows or the chickens or Caffy to think of . . . Things were a lot different then."

Her heavy hand stroked my cheek. "The angels have turned their faces from your family, these last few years. It began when that boy started digging and it's gone on from there."

I scowled. "Maybe Tin only started digging," I said, "because he knew the angels were about to turn away."

There was blasphemy somewhere in that, I suspected, but Mrs. Murphy didn't remark on it. She smiled at me sadly and said, "Poor child. Poor ignorant waif."

Da reckoned later that he could hear Mrs. Murphy gossiping from twenty miles away, could see her rapping on the neighbors' walls even with his eyes shut tight. She'd taken the lash of guilt to everybody's back, he claimed, like some mad crusading harpy. Why else would they tramp a path to our veranda, he asked, bringing buckets of milk and crates of vegetables?

"Perhaps they want to help us," said Mam.

"They pity us," said Da. "They pity us, and that's what I cannot bear."

"Look around you, Court. What do you have that makes you such a lordly man?"

For weeks afterward I don't believe they said a word to each other, Mam and Da, that wasn't said through gritted teeth, and we children scuttled to the outskirts to lurk leadenly, muted and aggrieved. Da refused to eat what the neighbors offered, and if Audrey cut Campbell pumpkin into our dinner he would fish the bits from his bowl and drop them splashing over to me. He would watch me eat it, his eyes glowing fiery and intent. He would not eat Robertson scones, though they came with fresh jam, or take Osborne milk in his tea. Soon he was eating almost nothing at all, and his flesh turned sallow and gray. He would sit gauntly at the table, his eyes following the arcs of our spoons. Audrey told me to take no notice but it was hard to find pleasure in the tang of dried apricot when Da reckoned it should taste bitter. "Are you enjoying that, Harper?" he would ask hoarsely. "That don't taste like poison to you?"

And the apricot would half choke me, would cling to my teeth with a strong nagging ache, and I'd run to the creek to rinse my mouth clean. I would drape my coat over the grass and curl up on it, my hands flat under my head. I tried, through those winter days, to stay away from the house as often as I could. Sometimes I went to the Godwins' and trailed after Izzy; sometimes I roamed the land alone, inspecting what caught my interest and swinging idly from branches of trees. I missed Tin, and looked for him wherever I was. I had not seen him for months. Gone, he became a bird in my mind, obliged to only the elements, owing undying thanks to none. Tin, I thought, had chosen the wisest way to live his life. I wished he had taken me with him.

The things Da said about the kindness of our neighbors did not wash off when Mam mopped the floor each Saturday morning, and it got so she could scarcely smile when she opened the door to another proffered pie. It ended the evening Lolly Fletcher stopped by, dangling a rabbit. It was a fine rabbit, sleek and hearty, and Da might have been pleased to have trapped it himself. But when Fletcher was gone we stared at the carcass and this time I didn't feel that distant grapple of trying to make sense of a thing: this time, I understood.

"Blast him." Da's voice was scratchy. "Does he mean that as an insult?"

Mam shook her head slowly. "Lolly's never been a cruel man."

"A rabbit." Da swore. "Do they think that I'm so daft I can't catch myself a rabbit?"

I frowned at him, perplexed. "Da, he's not meaning to hurt your feelings."

"What is his meaning, then? What's his meaning, if he's leading with my own suit?"

Audrey had her back to us; now she wheeled and made us jump. "Da!" she cried. "Are you blind?

The man gave us a rabbit because a rabbit is all he has! There's no meat in his larder, there's no vegetables in his ground! His children are hungry, same as yours! He's trying to help, but he doesn't have any more than we have—all he could give was something he could find, same way we might find it. He's as badly off as us, but he's doing his best, anyway, and you're not even grateful. I wish he'd rubbed your face in that goddamned rabbit."

Da was astonished and would have thrashed Audrey had she not been close to the door, and sharp to flee through it. She ran, her dress flying, and I tore after her. She must have heard me following and Mam hollering but she never stopped or looked around. She ran slower when we met the stony road and soon she was only marching and I let myself trot in her shadow. It was sundown and getting gloamy but I could see her face well enough to see she wasn't crying. I expected her to snap at me but she didn't bother. She didn't seem to care if I was alongside or not. So I hurried on, red dust icing on my feet and anxious to the pit of my stomach. Da hated us to give him cheek and Audrey was in for a ferocious whipping. I had never seen her get a whipping, and I never wanted to. Seeing it, I reckoned, would make nonsense of my whole world. "I'll take the strap for you," I said. "It wouldn't worry me."

She glanced down. "Da won't be strapping you or me."

After a time I asked, "Where are you going?"

"To see Izzy."

I supposed she was after consoling but she picked up a stick and jabbed it curtly into the road as she marched, and explained things to me.

"I'm going to tell Cable I'll be his housekeeper, if he still wants me. I haven't heard that he's changed his mind, so he may take me on. We'll have some money then, and Da will have no more reason to complain. He's making life a misery and I won't stand for it anymore. You'll have to cope without me, Harper, and I don't want to leave you, but things will be better for everyone this way. Better for people like Lolly Fletcher, too."

I could see there was no dissuading her so I didn't try, though my heart sank dismayed to my heels. And I could reluctantly understand it, her wanting to go.

Izzy Godwin had changed in the years he had spent on his uncle's land. He was still shy and soft-spoken but he didn't seem so breakable now, and his skin wasn't white as a lily. He wore his scarlet hair slicked neat behind his ears, and on his forearms he had several becoming scars. He was not so plain or coarse in his ways as most of the local boys, so all the ladies had eyes for him and would titter and be coy. He was kind and polite to each of them but Audrey was his favorite, and she was besotted with him. He was my best friend, I reckoned, but I had outgrown my childish shine.

Audrey came straight out and told him exactly what she meant to do. "I'll probably get one day a month to myself," she finished, "so I'll be able to see you when I come home. I doubt Mr. Cable will let you visit me there. I'll stay only as long as I must, until my family finds its feet."

We were standing in the yard of the Godwins, where Izzy had been digging manure into the kitchen garden. We could hear, from the kennels, the high-pitched yipping of greyhounds wanting their dinner. Izzy leaned against the fork, sighing. Audrey watched him through tired, steady eyes. Izzy looked at me, lingering on the veranda. "Harper," he said, "may I have a word with your sister in private?"

I obliged and took myself down the side of the house, though naturally not going so far away that I traveled out of earshot. I was an eavesdropper from my days with Tin beneath the shanty, it was my unholy habit, and I crouched without a ping of guilt at a place where I couldn't be seen. I heard Izzy jab the fork into the earth and then a long moment of silence and I held my breath cautiously. Listening without speaking or daring to move, as in those old days, put me in mind of Tin. I could almost feel him beside me, could nearly see him listening too.

"Audrey, do you know what people are saying about Vandery Cable?"

"No."

"They're saying it was him who took your cattle. That he hired those salesmen to do the job for him."

Audrey scoffed. "Oh, that's silly. That's just silly, Izzy."

"I'm only telling you what people are saying. It makes sense, in a way. Why didn't the men take Champion? A horse would have been useful to them, if they were ordinary thieves."

"Maybe they couldn't catch him. Champy was running free that night and he won't come to anyone but Devon."

"Maybe. But it still leaves you wondering how they disappeared as they did, despite herding three cows and all. That would have been easier to do with the help of someone like Cable."

Audrey mulled this over, and so did I. She asked, "But why would he do it? He said himself that the cattle were useless."

"They're saying it wasn't the cows he was after, that he got rid of them quick somehow. He didn't want the animals, you see—they were just his means to an end. That's why he didn't take Champion: he didn't need to, taking the cattle was enough. He's made it so you have to work for him, because now your family's got so much less than before. You refused him when you didn't really need him, so he made you have to change your mind."

Audrey was quiet. I heard the veranda creak as she sat down on it, and Izzy sat beside her. He said, "It makes sense, in a strange kind of way."

"It doesn't. There's no proof, none at all. It's a foolish rumor put about by people with nothing better to think about. And if Cable hears of it, he'll never take me on."

Izzy didn't answer but I reckoned he looked tenderly at her. I propped my forehead against the house, watching the meandering of some evening bug.

"I have to do it," Audrey said firmly. "We need the money. We need it desperately, Izzy. My father—we can't rely on him anymore. My mother has to be there for Harper. Devon must stay, to take care of things. It's only me who can do it. And I want to do it. I can't bear being home. It's horrible there now, and I hate the sight of everything I see. I need to be where things don't remind me. I need to go where Caffy can't find me. When you hear people spreading this story about Cable, tell them it isn't true. Will you do that, Izzy, please?"

"If you want me to," he said. "I'll do whatever you say."

I sat there while the night darkened from gloamy to pitch and nothing further was said, knowing that Audrey had forgotten me but not deeply minding. I didn't feel alone—I kept thinking that Tin was stretched out next to me and I kept being surprised to glance sideways and find he wasn't there. I was dozing in a bed of crushed treebark and leaves when Izzy shook me half awake and Audrey told me we were going home.

So Audrey packed her good dress and Mam cut up a handkerchief to make ribbons for her hair and Audrey went to Cable's just a week before I turned twelve. Da borrowed a mule and tray to take her and wouldn't let me come. I clung to her at the roadside, struggling not to cry. Da had said I was not to make a scene. The house seemed large and listless once she was gone, as though it pined for her. At nighttime I quaked under the covers, alone in the big bedroom. I remember the nights were windy then, and the roof of the house would rattle and groan. I was glad, in those days, to get up each morning and walk away to school, where I didn't have to think about anything. Things were too sad at home and I got to dreading the afternoon bell; I would linger, if I could, sweeping the floor or washing the boards, doing anything to avoid my fate. The teacher would be chafing, standing at the door shuffling books in his hands. On occasion I bedeviled him deliberately, so as an example to all rogues he kept me behind.

Some days, dawdling myself home, I would veer at Godwins' and stop awhile with Izzy, but he was always full of cheer, thinking that was what I needed. I preferred the sober company of Devon and wandered the surrounds with him, as I had done when I was a child. Champion would wander with us in his simple-minded horse's way. Devon had grown serious as he got older, and never wasted his words. It killed him that Audrey was working for Cable, but he hadn't tried talking to change her mind. I told him about the rumor of Cable and the cattle and he said he knew of it already. "What should we do?" I asked, but he didn't look at me and he didn't even answer. He plucked a snare from round a rabbit and took its front paws in his left hand, its rear paws in his right; he popped the creature's spine in an instant by jerking his hands apart. Mam was calling us for dinner, and we headed for the house. I knew he'd heard my question and I knew he was thinking, but it was useless to ask what he thought. He threw the rabbit on the step and we went inside. There was space round the table for everyone now, no one had to eat with their plate upon their knees. But at the table we sat uneasily, like dogs tied up together who aren't companions or friends.

Audrey came home at the end of the first month, looking much more contented than I wanted her to be. Cable's man delivered her to the door at midday and was due to collect her in the evening. Audrey wore a dress that she hadn't owned when she left us and she was carrying a quilted purse; slung at her elbow was a basket chocked with edibles. I was overjoyed to see her and hung around her neck while Mam brewed a pot of tea. "I make his breakfast and evening meal," she said, in answer to Mam's query. "He never eats at noon."

"Never eats at noon," Da echoed, full of admiration. He had been bustling about all morning, going to the door over and again to look for sign of Cable's jinker. Audrey's working for the pig farmer had turned Da into the cat that swallowed the canary. He was always talking about the things he would do now our Audrey had made something of herself.

"And it's such a big kitchen, and the storeroom has so many preserves on the shelves — I hardly knew where to start, when I first arrived. While Vandery's having breakfast, I make his bed and lay out his clothes for the day. Once a week I trim his hair and draw a bath. When he's left for the day, I dust or clean the windows and the rugs or I boil the clothes or polish the floor. In the early days I hardly had time to turn around, the house was in such a fusty state. There's been no woman on the property since his wife died, all those years ago. But everything's spick-and-span now, and sometimes there's nothing for me to do in the afternoon, so I borrow books from the study—Vandery said I may. I have my own room which looks on to the garden and it's nice to sit at the window and read in the sun."

Da's hands were under his chin. "Mr. Cable must be pleased. It sounds like he badly needed you."

"Vandery," said Devon. "Why do you call him that?"

Audrey looked a touch abashed. "He told me to. It's a habit now, I suppose."

Devon crooked an eyebrow; Mam leaned close and asked, "And he's treating you well, isn't he?"

"Oh, yes. Yes. I hope you're not worrying about me, Mam."

"Of course I am worrying about you—"

"Well, please don't."

Her eyes were skimming the room, not as if she were happy to see it and wanted to see things as fast as she could but as if what she saw made her eyes smart when she stopped and looked too long. She pressed her teeth into her lip, then smiled when she noticed us staring. "How have things been?" she asked, and took up her tea. "I think of you every day."

"Nothing has changed," Da said promptly. "You know our circumstances. It must be like a different planet, living at Mr. Cable's. A comfortable life and getting paid to boot. He's paying you properly, I trust?"

We knew what he was after. "Court," said Mam.

"What? I'm just thinking, I hope he's not trimming her wages for the time she spends reading in the sun."

Mam's face crumpled but Audrey squared her shoulders. From the quilted purse she tipped a handful of coins and laid them on the table. Da snatched them up and counted them. There wasn't much, I could see. He raised dark eyes to her.

"Is that all you're going to give us?"

"I'm sorry, Da. Mr. Cable said that, because I get my board and food, I can't expect much in wages."

Devon grimaced, disgusted. Da cradled the coins in his palm. "Just a little more?" he piped. "We're hungry here, Audrey. Just a touch more would set things right again. You're getting your keep for nothing, as you say, so you don't need to set aside anything for yourself—"

"I'm not keeping anything for myself." Her voice was stringy and pained. "I've given you all I got—"

"But this is a pittance! This is nothing! Where did you come by that new dress, I wonder? Dangling from a tree, was it?"

"Court, leave her—"

"Mr. Cable bought it! And that's all the money he gave me, every penny, I swear!"

Audrey's thin face was blazing and Da stared at her ferociously. He glanced at the purse but it was hanging limp. He pushed the coins into his pocket and didn't say another word. Over lunch Audrey picked at her meal, eating hardly anything, and between snips of stuttering conversation the air was tight and twanged. Afterward she went to see Izzy and I paced about dejectedly until she returned, convinced she was gone forever, knowing I couldn't blame her if vanishing were the thing she chose. I hated Da that afternoon, loathed him like I could have run him through with pokers. I wished he would disappear instead, so I'd never have to see him again.

But Audrey did come home, when Devon and I were in the paddock, chipping stones to pass the time, and she walked out to meet us where we sat on a wind-smoothed mullock heap. I shaded my eyes against the sun and said, "I'll never forgive Da for what he said to you."

"Harper, don't be like that."

She was just a silhouette to me, with shafts of sunlight spilling off her. "He was mean," I said. "He should have been glad to see you, but all he wanted to be was mean. He used to be kind, but now he never is. Ever since the day the shanty fell down he's been mean, mean, mean."

"It didn't happen like that," said Devon. He was chipping at a pebble that was shot through with color and didn't look up from this work. "You're too young to remember. He's always been mean — before the shanty, and after it. He's always been a coward. The shanty just gave him something to blame for his being mean and cowardly. Now he's only happy if he's got a flask to cling to and someone to make miserable."

"He went to the war, though," mused Audrey.

"He must have been brave once."

"You know the story. He went to the war because he was afraid of Grandda."

I was silent, recalling this was true. And felt sorry for my Da.

Audrey dipped a hand down the front of her dress and brought out a fold of notes. There were only four of them and they were only small but they made my eyes bulge as if she'd performed some stupendous magic trick. She passed them to me, saying, "Take this, Harper, and hide it where Da won't find it. He'll waste the money I gave him, so give this to Mam. Just make sure that Da doesn't see."

I took the money and tucked it under me. The three of us sat with our faces in the breeze. Far off we could see the house with the dogs skulking by the door and the post of the clothesline blown over on the ground.

"So you like working for Cable." Devon knocked a splinter from the stone and brushed the grit aside.

"I have to make the best of it."

"Maybe." He polished the pebble with a licked finger. "But you don't have to call him by his first name. It makes me feel sick to hear."

Audrey sighed, putting her chin in her hands. "I

have to do as he says, Devon. If I want to earn a living, that's the way things must be. He tells me to call him Vandery, so I do. I eat my dinner at his table because he told me to, he says he likes a lady's manners. He asks me to read to him and I can feel his eyes crawling over me but I read to him, anyway. He makes me trim his hair and I need to stand close to do it, I can feel him breathing on my skin. He watches me and he uses every excuse to touch me or be touched by me and being shut in the same house with him repels me—but Harper can hide the money now, and I'll keep my mind on that."

I was confused, I didn't understand what she was saying, I didn't know why Devon snarled, "I'm going to kill him, I swear."

"Don't. Promise me, Devon, stay away and mind your business. He's a lonely man, and he doesn't mean any harm. I can take care of myself, and we need the money."

Devon stared at her and she stared at the house and I looked swiftly, stupidly, from one of them to the other, floundering beneath that glassy surface I had never quite broken through. Audrey said hoarsely, "Give the money to Mam when Da's not home, Harper. I should go—I've got to go."

But she didn't go; she stayed toying the stones and warming in the breeze until we saw the jinker jambling up the hill with the man slouched in its seat and the whip clenched in one hand and the reins held taut in the other.

It wasn't long after that, less than a fortnight I suppose, that we woke up and found Devon gone. The day previous he had ridden off on Champion and returned so late that Mam and Da were already sleeping and I was reading in bed. Mr. Robertson's girl Georgina had outgrown a batch of storybooks and passed them on to me to read, but mostly I looked at the pictures. There was one about the seaside and the drawings entranced me. I had never seen the ocean, I'd never even considered it before. There was no space for that much water in my head, for an entire unknown landscape. But whether perusing the pictures or whispering the words, I wasn't allowed to use candles at night for anything other than visiting the privy, so when I heard the door swing I had snuffed the flame and hidden the book and lay with my hands over my nose and mouth, listening to the boards creak beneath Devon. He paused in the door of my bedroom and I clamped closed my eyes. "Harper," he said. "I know you're awake."

I had opened my eyes and peered at him. He was almost lost in the dimness but I could see his fair hair glint in the haze coming off the embers. "Where have you been, Devvy?"

"Round and about. I saw Tin."

"Did you? How is he?"

"He's a savage. He nearly didn't stop, though he knew it was only me. He bares his teeth like an animal does when it's cornered. He's just a wild thing now."

He came forward, struck a match and lit the candle. I sat up on an elbow and blinked at him. His face was smudgy, his hair was in his eyes. He looked tired and his clothes were smirched but he stood straight and steady and from him came the strengthening smell of the horse's sweat and hay. "You can have the light, if you want it," he said. "This is a big room, to be alone inside."

"I'm not afraid," I answered smartly. "I was reading a book. Have you ever seen the ocean, Devvy?"

"No, I don't reckon."

"I would like to see it."

"Well, maybe you will one day."

I smiled, rubbing my goose-bumped arms. "I was reading a book," I repeated. "I'm not afraid."

He nodded somberly down at me. "That's good. It's good, that you're brave. You shouldn't let yourself be frightened, Harper. People who let themselves be frightened, they're defeated before they've even tried. Being cowardly never changed anything. It's being brave that makes the difference."

I had frowned at him, suspecting he'd been drinking, speaking gibberish like he was. But when he bent and kissed my cheek I hadn't sniffed alcohol and that puzzled me even more. In my experience men only talked heart-sore blitherings when they'd been hitting the bottle. I should have asked him what he meant but when he left the room I hadn't stopped him. I had not liked it, him being strange.

And the next morning, he was gone. His bed hadn't been slept in, so perhaps he had only waited until I'd fallen asleep before crossing the threshold again. While he'd waited he had packed a swag with most of what he owned. Then he'd written and sealed a letter, leaving it in the pocket of Mam's apron where Da wouldn't find it but Mam's hand would settle on it before she got the fire going. I woke to hear her calling him as loud as her voice could go. I hurried to see what was happening and found her in the yard, staring into the distance with her arms hung limp and the letter caught in her fingertips, kickering in the breeze. She didn't look at me. "Devon's gone," she said, and her voice was dead as stone. "Another one, gone."

I took the letter and read it and then I was running through the grass for the animal shelter, snagging and tearing my nightdress as I dodged between the fence rails. Champion was not in the shelter and his saddle, rug, halter, and bridle were gone. I ran to the peak of the highest mullock heap and scanned the paddock for the horse's lanky form. "Devon!" I wailed. "Champion! Here, horse! Champy! Devon!"

I yelled the words again, though I knew that doing so was childish. I knew Devon wouldn't have lied. I gripped the hem of the nightdress and wiped my stinging eyes. I turned back toward Mam, who was standing like a statue in the soft swirling dust of the yard. She still wasn't looking at me. I was the only one left to watch but she was looking out over the hill, to where the others had gone.

When Devon had left the house the day before, he had ridden Champion into town and sold the horse and the gear to the stock agent. Doing so must have made him ache in every bone, for he had loved that creature. I remembered him once saying that Champ could understand him and I wondered if, as he rode, he had explained things to the horse or whether he had been silent instead, keeping his friend in ignorance till the last. He had walked home in Champion's hoofprints, which were still visible on the empty road, and the length of the journey and the dragging chain on his heart were what made him so late getting home. He'd put the money from the sale into an envelope and then written the letter, scrawling Mam's name when everything was done.

He had left in the dead of night so he would be well on his way by sunrise and no one would be around to stop him from doing what he intended to do. He was going to tramp the countryside, picking up whatever work he could find. He would go far from town, far from the scavenged haunts of the traveling salesmen, to places so remote that his chances must improve. Someone somewhere would employ him, maybe with a logging job, and give him a wage he could depend upon. In the meantime he wanted Audrey to stop housekeeping for Vandery Cable. We didn't need her earnings now we had the money from Champion. We could make it last, Devon thought, long enough for him to find work and start sending money home. There were four crossed kisses at the bottom of the letter and a postscript warning us to keep the money hidden from Da. Mam flopped as if the earth was pulled from under her and, startling me, she cried.

Later that day we realized he'd taken one of the younger of the old dogs along with him and I was pleased to know it, pleased he wasn't alone.

The next day Da rode the Osbornes' mule to town to try to buy Champion back. Nothing would console Mam but that the horse should be ours again, and I was astonished when Da agreed. "The boy shouldn't have done it." He paced about, muttering. "There was no need for this, no need at all." He had an expression on his face as if he'd been drenched in water.

But Champion could not be bought back, though I soundly believe Da tried. The agent had sold the horse on already. Devon had been making inquiries; he'd heard there was a cattle drive skirting town. He'd asked the dealer if the stockmen would be interested in a solid beast like Champion. The dealer had reckoned they might be, so he bought the horse from Devon and took him over to the campsite that evening. Champion had been sold for the second time in a day and the drovers, with Devon's pet carrying their packs across his speckled shoulders, were now miles gone.

Mam and I sat with bowed heads while we listened to this story. The tale was tangled like a moth in a web and I think, looking back, that Devon intended it that way. He wanted Champ to be so irretrievable that he could spare himself from hoping.

The money he had put in the envelope was lying crumpled on the table and Da stared at it dismally. "It's blood money, this," he said, and pushed it away. My lip was trembling, thinking of Champion. He had always been noble and beautiful, the most beautiful thing we ever owned. I hoped the drovers would look after him, treat him kindly, scratch between his ears where he liked it, remember he was aging, and not make him carry too weighty a load.

Mam said raspily, "We must bring Audrey home, Court."

Da nodded gravely, saying, "That is what he wanted."

But Audrey, when Da traveled out to collect her, smiled tenderly. "You sound as if Devon has died," she told him. "Devon isn't dead, and my leaving here isn't his dying wish. Plenty of young men have struck out to find work, Da—there's no need to be so miserable."

"Maybe it wasn't his dying wish, but it must have almost killed him selling that horse. He did it so you could come home."

Audrey sighed, leaning against the veranda's ornate railing-post. She was not wearing an apron or anything that would make her look the house-maid. "Devon never thinks things through prop-erly," she said, a little tetchily. "So many men are on the road, searching for work. What if he doesn't find anything for months? What if he has to wan-der from house to house, bartering for scraps? He won't be sending anything home while he's doing that, and the money from Champion will dwindle away. We'll have nothing again, like we had before. I don't want that. I don't want Mam and Harper going hungry. I don't want the neighbors looking out for us. You don't want it either, Da. The sen-sible thing is for me to stay here until Devon finds something secure."

"But Cable pays you almost nothing, anyway—"

"He's going to pay me more now," she said quickly. "I'll be able to give you more, at the end of this month."

"What your daughter says is sense, Flute." It was Cable's voice, making Audrey and Da wheel. He was standing in the doorway smoking a thin cigar, more like a lord than a farmer. "Even you must be capable of seeing that. Just because you get a puddle of money doesn't mean you should earth in the stream."

Da had scraped his hat from his head and clutched it tightly. "It was what Devon wanted, Mr. Cable. I'm only telling her what Devon wanted."

"He wants his sister to give up learning a reliable occupation. He wants her to be helpless, forever at the mercy of others to get whatever she needs. That appears to me to be what Devon wants for her."

"I see your point, sir," Da conceded. "But I'm just telling Audrey —"

"Besides," Cable added, blowing a feather of smoke, "I don't reckon you can afford much, Flute, when it comes to weddings. A bride can't wear a flour sack, and you can't feed guests on thin air. Young Godwin hasn't much to show for himself, so your daughter's in need of every shilling."

Da swung with confusion to Audrey, and Audrey blushed purple. "You're marrying Izzy Godwin?"

She mumbled and twisted. "Maybe one day. One day I might."

Cable was grinning vastly. He flipped the dregs of his cigar spinning over the railing. "So you see, Flute," he chortled, "Audrey can't possibly leave now."

Mam and I listened stunned to this tale, both of us truly dumbfounded. I knew, without knowing how I knew it or recalling when I came to learn it, that Izzy did not love Audrey as much as she loved him, and that Audrey had the pitiable habit of believing otherwise. Mam's eyes were wide with surprise: she asked, "Did Audrey say Izzy's agreeable to this?"

"Why wouldn't he be, Thora? He could do worse. Audrey's a good girl—sensible, too. She's always been sensible. That's sense, about waiting until Devon gets a job before chucking in her own."

Mam shook her head. "What I mean is, I've never thought of Izzy Godwin as the marrying kind."

Da wasn't listening. His gaze had rambled over to me and his hand came up to ruffle my hair, something he hadn't done in years. "Chicken," he said, "that dress you're wearing is tatty, and you're breaking out of the seams. It's time you had a new one."

"Don't waste the money, Da," I said cautiously. "We have to remember not to waste it, don't we? We should be careful about what we buy."

He burst out laughing. "Did you hear that, Thora?" he cried. "What's made you into such a worrying old woman, Harper?"

I glanced at Mam, who was staring vacantly through the open window. Da was chuckling and flicking me on the nose. I felt a touch of giddy madness, a bee buzzing in my brain. I didn't know, anymore, when I should be happy. I'd forgotten, I realized, when was the proper time to smile.

So began my life as an only child and the boredom grated upon me until I would rush up the rise of a mullock heap with the dogs swarming around me and lift my chin and howl, setting all the dogs for miles arguing and raging and the birds exploding into the air like gunshot, bounding with bare feet over stones that jabbed the soles and hurt so much that I saw stars, doing all this just to get some commotion into my existence, some reaction to my being alive. We had chickens again and for the first time we owned a milking cow, but my home that hot summer had had the aliveness skimmed from it. Wherever I stood there was land sloping in every direction, so much land I could never see the end of it, but sometimes I felt I was living in a tiny crate and that the air oozing through the breathing-holes was never enough to let me satisfactorily fill my lungs.

I put the money Audrey had given me into a jar and buried it in the brown earth near the creek, marking the place with a stone. Audrey had told me to give it to Mam, but I didn't. I wanted to save it until we needed it badly, and every day I thought I saw that occasion stalking closer. Mam and Da had gone to town with the money from Champion and brought home the chickens and the strawberry cow; for me they had sandals and a dress, the first I'd ever owned that hadn't been owned by someone before. My blood had chilled at the sight of the cow, my guts jerked like they'd been hooked. We didn't need a dairy cow, it being cheap to buy milk by the pail, and her price had wasted over half the money. Mam seemed pleased to own her—she seemed as proud as Da. I saw a stingy redness behind my eyes and ran to the creek, where I had used rocks to dam a shady pool. The water was deep enough to soak me and it was the only place in my world that was cool. I sat still while a marchfly drilled its probe into my ankle, sucking back tears in an agony of worry that my Mam had followed the dark path taken by my Da.

That was the summer I was twelve years old.

Audrey came home at the end of her second month working for Cable; I had been eager to see her through the weeks leading up to her visit but on the day itself I was in an irate temper, my brains banging wrathfully at my skull, and I squirmed with aggravation as she talked about life on the hog farm. Her duties were lighter now that Cable had dismissed his station hand, who was accused of being too fond of the silver. The man's departure left only Audrey and Cable on the property, along with the pigs. She was raising a runt and its neediness filled the hours. The piglet interested me but not very much, and I wandered into the yard. The heat hit like a swung plank and I stood there with my scalp burning, surly and sluggish and fuming. I wanted to ask about the daydream wedding and then laugh like a crow when Audrey's smile was wiped away. I wanted the weather to break and storm. I wanted not to be angry; I wanted my whole life to begin again. I kicked at the dirt and snarled and the dogs in the shade dropped their ears and blinked appeasingly at me. I would stay in this place forever and every hour would be the same. My brothers and sister had escaped, having made that leap of courage, but I never, ever would. I did not think I lacked courage but I suspected there was no far side for me to land on, were I to try a leaping too. I was left behind unwanted, there was no need or use for me. I felt my fury turning like a whirligig, full of muck and broken litter. *Why did you have me?* I wanted to demand of Mam. Why raise me, feed me, keep me, if my life was going to be lived in a cage?

And then sometimes, between black fits of thunder, I would curl into Mam's lap and she would tell a tale or sing a lullaby and I would feel nothing but tranquil, like a child, and loved.

I felt the weight of the daylit hours like a millstone dragging after me, especially once school finished for the year. I had never been a good student, being a chatterer, a notorious distracterer, and lazy. My knuckles were tough from the times the whiplash cane had striped them and the very sight of my lesson books never failed to disquieten my stomach. But those lonely days wanted more filling than lurking alone could provide and I started reluctantly to read. I rifled through the castoffs given me by Georgina Robertson, swiping past the drawings of the ocean until I found the improving tales of sterling boys and virtuous girls. I did not like the virtuous girls, thinking them embarrassingly wet and holy. The sterling boys were smug as goats. Devon had said I was brave; I was a brave girl and I wanted to read stories about a brave girl who could possibly be mistaken for me. I searched through all the books without finding her but I was not discouraged, I simply took up a pencil myself. In my heart I understood that only I had the expertise to record the adventures of this particular girl.

I had no paper, so I wrote my first story over the blank end pages of the books. In that story the heroine could fly, and I came to envy and soon resent her. Mrs. Murphy gave me a sheaf of butcher's wrapping and on this I grounded my next creation, plucking wings with pleasure; I liked this girl much better. All summer I populated the house with one valiant young lady after another, sheets of paper spilling from beneath my lead-stained hands.

But between each painstakingly handwritten tale and in between milking the cow and sweeping the floor and scrubbing the pots and wringing the clothes and between the sleepy evenings snuggled awkwardly across my mother's lap, I whiled away the days moping and brewing discontent. It makes me sad now, to know I let so much time pass by unappreciated. I wasn't going to stay there, in that place I'd lived a lifetime, for very much longer. I try to forgive myself because I didn't know about it then. If I had known, I would have tried to inscribe things more deeply in my memory. And I would have made myself be cheerful, too, because you can always make the effort to savor the final moments of anything.

Audrey crashed through the door while I was at the table bent over a book, waving away a wasp with one hand and, with the other, feeding myself from a plate of honey pikelets. Blasts of morning air were gusting through the unglassed window and the pages were crimping with the heat of it, and when the door swung back for Audrey the whole book went jagging across the table. She stumbled forward and stood reeling, her face ashen, her eyes raw. "Audrey," I muttered, and, sensing the problem was bigger than me, began yelping for my Mam.

She came charging from the shelter and Da came, too, hearing from off in the paddock. I sprang to the window but couldn't see a dust cloud raised by any vanishing jinker. If Audrey had walked home it would have taken her hours, especially in the treachery of night. Audrey had collapsed at the table by now, her hair damp and stringy and her hands flat to her eyes. Mam had knelt beside her and Da stood patting her back ungainedly. "What's happened?" he kept asking. "Audrey, Audrey, what's wrong?"

She suddenly started crying, as if Da were jolting tears out each time he patted her. Mam waved him aside and he and I stood by the wall, hacking at our fingernails. Mam reached to Audrey and lifted up her chin. Until that moment everything had been unfathomable and I'd been hopping with excitement, my kneecaps positively quivering. But when I saw the swollen eyes that turned to meet Mam's and the dull glaze of a blow across my sister's cheek, the whole room tilted, I felt woozy with the horror. When Audrey saw Mam, whose tired lovely face was creased with concern, a sob came from her as if everything inside had been slashed brutally through.

"Audrey," Mam murmured, steady and serene, "tell me."

She shook her head violently, hiding her face with her arms. Mam glanced at Da, whose eyes were round and huge. To Audrey she said, "Please. I can't bear to see you weeping."

Audrey hunched tighter, her fists caught cruelly in her hair. She pounded her feet on the boards as though she hoped to smash them through. She gasped for air and struggled and stamped, having a fit of hysteria. But Mam calmed her gradually, cradling Audrey to her and saying downy, soothing words. By the time Audrey uncovered her eyes, both Da and I had turned white as sheets. "Make Harper go," she sighed, and though her words were slow and sodden I heard them and went, carefully closing the door.

Outside the sun was searing and the dogs nowhere to be seen. I put my ear to the door at once but the house had many deficiencies in regard to eavesdropping, the golden wood being thick and strong. I ducked instead to where the wadding had crumbled and left a slivery gap, which gave me the narrowest view. Mam and Audrey had their backs to me, and Da was keeping his head bowed.

Audrey choked out her story. I could only hear the odd word. *Cable. Drinking. Dinner. Dress.* Mam held Audrey's wrist, as if to stop her escaping. *That Godwin boy's a nancy, a queer, he's never marrying you. Think of the good you could do for your family. No one needs to know.*

Mam covered her mouth with her apron; Da put

a hand to his heart. I crushed my ear against the house, straining to catch the words.

I can't — I won't — let me go!

My skin was prickling, stinging in the sun.

Stop. Floor. Noise. Ran. What will people say? What will people say?

Audrey's forehead hit the table, making Mam and me flinch. Da crossed the room in an instant, snatching up the gun. "Put the rifle down, Court," Mam snapped at him. "That is not the way."

I heard the rifle click neatly as Da checked the slug that had waited unused so long in the barrel. "I'm sorry, Thora," he answered, "but something has to be done."

"For God's sake, Court —"

"Da, don't, stay here —"

"No!" he barked, and I wish I could have seen him truly for I believe he stood taller than he'd ever stood before, tall and straight and dignified. "That man needs to be taught respect."

"You'll make everything worse!"

"Da, he has a rifle, too!"

"Audrey," he said, calm and firmly, "something must be done."

He made for the door and I rushed to be there when he opened it, grappling for his arm. He swept past me, the rifle lashing in his hand, striding for the road. Mam dashed a distance after him, and I after her. "Court," she was begging, "please!"

He didn't look at her, didn't slow himself down. Mam stopped with a choking cry, her hands out to the air. She spun back toward the house, in anguish over Audrey. She saw me then, and yanked me to her. "Go with your father," she hissed. "Don't let him lose his head."

I obeyed instantly, sprinting after my Da. He was marching swiftly, the old war wound that had lamed him for years suddenly seeming healed. I stayed some paces behind him, wary of making a sound. My mind was swimming, uncertain what to do. I didn't understand what Audrey had meant, in the kitchen; I wasn't sure what Da intended to do with the gun. I knew we were walking to Cable's and that was miles away. I had the ghastly creeping feeling that my Da was going to die.

He knew I was trailing him but never slowed or threw a word. Now and then he muttered to himself but said not a word to me. We weren't walking on the road but through the scrub that scribbled along it, and no one looking for us would have seen. Da pushed aside whippy branches and they sprang away after him, catching me in the chin; my bare legs were soon scratched bloody. Bush flies darted around us, diving for our mouths and eyes; stray locusts leaped from the bracken, startling me each time. I kept my sights on Da, though, on the sweat bathing his slim brown neck, on the blackness soaking his shirt.

It was late afternoon when we reached the boundary of Cable's property, and I was staggering with exhaustion. Da squatted behind a tree and studied the homestead intently, the rifle rearing over his shoulder. Now was the time to say something eloquent but my throat was parched as a skeleton and my brain was sputtering with fatigue. "Dadda," I mumbled, "please come home."

After all those hours of following him, he finally looked at me. I was kneeling beside him and he smiled and tapped my nose. His thin face was grimy, his brow was torn and seeping, and there was a leaf caught up in his wispy hair. "Chicken," he said. "You've always been my chicken."

I nodded dumbly, my eyes sizzling in my skull. "It's not safe here, Da. Come home to Mam and me."

"I can't, chicken."

"But I'm afraid."

"There's nothing to fear. Mr. Cable and I just mean to exchange a word or two."

"Then leave the gun here, and I'll take care of it."

"I'll need the gun, chicken. Folk like Mr. Cable haven't much respect for words. He doesn't respect people, so why would he respect their words?"

I shook my head wretchedly. Tears were dribbling down my cheeks. Da used his cuff to smear them away. "You head off home," he told me. "Go and take care of your sister and Mam. In the morning you'll wake up proud of your Da."

"I don't want to—Da, don't go! Stay, Da, don't go, don't, Da—Da!"

But he was going, cleaving through the grass, angling for the homestead. I watched him moving farther and farther away from me. I scanned, desperately, for help: one of the neighbors should have been there, to wrestle the rifle away. But everything was silent and the only living things nearby were the birds and the gnats that hopped onto my skin, and Da and the rumble of Cable's hogs.

Da was at the door now, hammering. I couldn't sit useless a moment longer—I pounced up and ran, bounding over the grass tussocks, hollering his name and anything else I could think of, bellowing at the power of my voice. I don't know what I thought I was doing, except maybe aiming for confusion.

But Da was still at the door when I got to him, and nobody had opened it. I flung my arms around his waist but he paid no attention to me. He shuffled to the window and peered inside. He swore then, frustrated. He pried me off and started for the rear of the house and I scrambled, once more, after him.

As soon as we rounded the building, Da stopped in his tracks. There was a drizzle of blood on the courtyard stones. It was dry blood, a string of tawny drops. The back door of the house was open and Da hoisted the rifle. The noise of the pigs, their scoffs and shattering squeals, could be heard much louder from here, though their pens were far away. "Cable," Da called, lifting his voice above the din. "Vandery Cable, are you there? I want a word with you."

When there was no answer after a moment or two he stepped over the threshold, and I glided after him. He pivoted, all of a sudden, and pushed me roughly outside. "Damn, Harper," he snarled,

"I told you to go. Get home, I'm telling you."

I cowered, watching fretfully as he hedged into the unlit room and then turned a corner and out of my sight. I gripped the door frame and chewed my lip, waiting and listening. I couldn't hear Da moving about anywhere. The sun had lanked my hair and strands were sticking to my throat. I stared down at the droplets, the cobblestones like mirrors reflecting the setting sunlight. There was more blood than I had first noticed, a spray of ruby speckles as if someone had shaken their dripping hands. The yard was enclosed by whitewashed shacks that were flaring brightly and I tracked the drops curiously to the door of one of them. There was no wind but the door was wavering on its hinges. I pushed it back and looked inside. What I saw startled me, but not enough to make me yell.

From beams in the ceiling dangled hooks and from each hook hung the hefty carcass of a pig, three of them in all. The carcasses were caught by the tendons in their legs, and their sloped heads, their furrowed snouts and fringed pink ears, were pointed at the ground. Each pig had been slit down the belly and the insides were scooped-out caverns; globules of creamy fat were oozing from the wounds. The flesh of the pigs was blue and pallid and the tails flopped over the chunky buttocks, having lost their twirl. The eyes were the strangest thing, little white balls bulging between the eyelids as if at any moment they would pop clear away. I stepped into the room and stood among them, daring myself to touch one. The air was rancid and there was blood splashed everywhere, over the walls and on the pigs themselves. This wasn't ancient blood, from hogs slain in the past; these three hogs had been alive this morning, and this blood was clotted and fresh. A matting of flies was sipping at it and did not stir on seeing me, stupid with the pleasure.

I heard the smallest noise and glanced at my feet. The floor of the shack was strewn with bloody sawdust and beneath this was wood. Silly, I wanted to tell Cable, to have a wood floor in a hanging room. Dirt would have been better, although not so fancy. Blood is wet and surely ruins wood; in time he'd find his fine floor all buckled up and useless. Already it felt spongy and weak beneath my weight.

Then came that tiny sound again, so meek it should have meant nothing and only got my attention because I was just then looking at the floor.

What happened next must have happened in a flicker but to me things moved so slowly I saw everything in its separate moment, as frozen as those sketches of the sea. A hole opened in the floor directly beneath me, opened downward like a lid leading into the earth, and I dropped through and tumbled, knowing as I went that I was falling into Tin's tunnels and that the trap door in the floor of Cable's hanging room had been cut there by my brother, that feral thief.

I rolled and thumped and then I was just flying, feeling nothing above or below or to the sides of me and seeing nothing either, not even the square of light from the open trap door. I knew I was falling a long way and that each somersault and slithering was taking me farther from where I ever wanted to be. I started a desperate yowling, more panicked than in pain. Standing knock-kneed in Cable's glaring yard was a preferable place to be.

And then I was sprawled to a stopstill on a pile of cushioning dirt, the air walloped out of me and my wails instantly silenced. I fought to get my breath back, gasping and gathering myself in a ball. The darkness of the place petrified me; I couldn't see a thing, not even a hand in front of my face. I made to stand and my head hit the ceiling and dropped me promptly down again, where I sat gripping my ankles and grizzling. I didn't know which way I had come and the walls, when I put a hand to them, seemed sheer on every side. I didn't know which direction would lead me to the trapdoor; disoriented and blinded, I could not sense which way was up and, for all that I knew, I might be standing on my head. I was knocked and bruised all over and my dress and arms were damp. It made me think there must be water leaking in and the thought of drowning in the tunnels galvanized me with fear. I lifted my chin and roared. "Da! Dadda!" And clutched my ears because my voice became mammoth in the narrow confines of the tunnel and boomed around me, not like an echo but like a circling, screeching, ridiculing wraith. It didn't travel anywhere but stayed close, mockingly. I hugged my knees tightly, my chin hunkered to my chest. My situation was dire. If Da could not hear me, he wouldn't know what had happened; if he couldn't see me, he would not trouble to look for me. Not seeing or hearing me, he would think I had gone home, just as he had told me. I might sit in the tunnel forever if I didn't get myself out.

I don't know for how long I huddled there; I remember it seemed an age before I had the courage to shuffle forward warily. Tin had a labyrinth of tunnels, everyone knew. He could appear anywhere, and disappear. If he could do that there must be many entrances and exits to this underground jungle and if I searched for them, with a bit of luck I would find one. I squinted once more for light shining past the trapdoor but the tunnel must have kinked or corkscrewed because I was crouched in pitchness as heavy as a wet woolen coat. I felt the walls around me, gauging the space I was in, sliding my fingers along the slick floor of the tunnel and wincing at the touch of tickling roots and fibers. Clods of earth plipped onto my head and made my heart leap every time but I told myself to stay calm. I'm brave, I reminded myself: I'm a brave girl. It's dark and I'm lost but worse could have happened, this isn't very bad.

Dogs, wandering freely, go uphill, and that's a thing that makes sense. I had fallen down and the way out would be to go up. I slunk to my belly and tried to fathom which was higher, my chin or my toes. Neither felt different from the other. Both felt exactly the same. The place where I was lying seemed perfectly flat. "Da," I moaned despairingly, pressing my cheek to the earth and sobbing with the tragedy.

But soon I lifted my head again, wiping away my tears. I thought of the exits and how many there must be. I shook myself and drew a deep breath and began crawling, in the direction I was facing, forward on my hands and knees.

I kept my eyes open, I don't know why. Tin's eyes had grown huge from his years in the darkness but mine were accustomed to daylight and I couldn't see a thing. I fought against the blackness every moment, but I stayed as sightless as if I'd been born without eyes. I trundled forward, my fingers furled into fists, my knees and knuckles thickening with wet cold earth that clung. My teeth were closed so tight they ached, and I hissed through them tune-lessly to keep myself company. Like finches hearing gunshot all thoughts fled my head as soon as I was moving, leaving behind them a rustling, empty space. Maybe, if my mind had chattered and cart-wheeled, I would still be down there. But there was a saving brainlessness inside me: I had arms and legs and all my effort went into using them. I was moving, I was clawing, I was not sitting rigid and waiting to die.

My head smacked a wall and dropped me on my haunches. Panic shrieked through me and was gone. I fumbled to either side and understood that I was at a smoothly curving intersection and needed to choose my way. I sat still, peering for light, listening for sound, and hideous thoughts flocked like crows to a corpse and fear welled up in an instant, slamming into my heart. I jolted forward, scrambling down the closer tunnel. I would not stop again, I swore: I would not pause and let myself consider. Moving kept the dread at bay, and moving would keep me alive. But I had chosen my tunnel badly: this one was smaller and my head grazed the ceiling, my elbows scraped the floor, I had to slip to my belly and wiggle like a worm in my efforts to get through.

I came soon to another crossways, and very soon another. Sometimes I had to choose between three or four directions and I made the decision without care or calculation. My head ached from the times it struck the roof, my backbone was missing skin from when it had done the same. My kneecaps cracked on invisible rocks, and tree roots netted my fingers and legs. It was cool in the tunnels but it was warm work getting along them and my jaws unlocked to pant noisily. There was no breeze, and no smell to the air that wasn't the ancient smell of earth—there was nothing I could sniff that might show me the way. My muscles were hurting, my eyeballs were smarting from the strain of trying to see. I blundered and lurched forward, crippled by a flourishing sympathy for myself. My bottom lip wobbled; my voice came out as a gurgle and I sounded like a baby. I formed the words with difficulty, like someone who's never spoken before. "Help me," I gagged pitifully. "Help me, help me."

I shouldn't have said it, because the sound awoke my sluggish brain. Before I could catch it my mind had bolted screaming, hauling me along a path as sunless and sinister as the tunnels themselves.

It began with thoughts of Caffy—Caffy, like me, in the ground. In the ground now, after a lonely little funeral with just the few people who had known him to bid him goodbye. Caffy had always cried so sorrowfully at night, made forlorn in the darkness: now he, like me, lay buried in blackness, cold to the sun and blind to its rays. But Caffy had been in the ground before that, too, entombed in the well. In the grave he slept in the arms of angels but he had been awake and alone down that well, and crying, afraid. I had never let myself think of the terror he would have known down there and when such thinking stalked near me I'd do anything, anything, to make it go away. Now though, in the tunnels, the thoughts shook me like a dog shakes a rat and my mind spun agonized, my ears began to ring. What happened to Caffy had been my fault— I was the only one who could properly be blamed. He was just a baby and I had sent him to a place where he would slowly die, all the time cursing him and cross with him and wishing he would be quiet. And he was quiet, in the end; when we found him, his mouth was full of dirt. Had he been able to hear Tin coming closer and had he opened his mouth to shout with excitement, to yell for Tin to hurry? Or had the noise of Tin's claws plowing toward him made him shudder, and had his last sounds been whimpers of dismay? Because Caffy had always been frightened of Tin, who had never seemed familiar, who had looked like a wild animal then and truly was one now, a wild thing not just in face and figure but deep in his heart, too, wild. No one had been down the well with Caffy, so no one knew what Tin had seen when he'd broken through at last, into the well. We simply supposed he had seen a boy already dead. But maybe he had seen a child reaching gladly out to him, or a child not dead but dying? Maybe he saw a child die of horror just to see him—or maybe he saw a child who could be easily made to die. Because Mrs. Murphy always said Tin had his resentments against Caffy. I had always argued vehemently that what she said was wrong. Now, all of a sudden, I felt sick with apprehension. My blood banged and squirted fiercely in my veins. Tin was wild, much more so than he had been when he dug for Caffy. He wouldn't come near us anymore, he wouldn't answer to our calls. He took flight if anyone came too close to him and like any untame creature he might fight the one who threatened him. Tin: there was less that was human in Tin than there were bits of something else. He was not a boy, but an unowned and willful animal. He had claws and teeth and a territory he must defend, and I was lost within it. And I knew then, as if I'd heard him whisper, that he was close and watching me.

That was the moment when I knew what Tin had done. None of the words for it came to my mind but I knew as sure as if the knowledge had been in my head for a lifetime and was just now draining through. Thoughts fitted into each other like a tidy chain of pawprints left behind a cat. I remembered the blood on the pigs, fresh sometime that morning; I remembered the emptiness of Cable's home, not empty as if he'd just stepped out but empty as if he'd never lived there. And every atom of me shriveled because Tin could do it, for sure: he had done it once and maybe twice and I was helpless in his labyrinth, where he could easily do it again. Maybe he would do it because I was trespassing and he didn't recognize me—I hadn't seen him for the longest time. But maybe he would recognize me, because there had been times when I thought he saw me, although I could not see him—and maybe he would do it anyway.

I sped, then, as if speed should save me. I plunged headlong into the blackness, my knees slipping from under me and limbs tangling up with each other, my chin hitting the earth when my haste toppled me. I knew I would not escape him, not even if I could stand and run. I was used to the sky over my head and rangy open spaces and in the warren I was hampered, pathetically clumsy, a living thing thrown into a pinched catacomb. But this knowledge didn't stop me from powering feverishly onward, colliding and collapsing and hauling myself to my hands and knees. Pain shrilled from a hundred places on me and I was wheezy with the dust in the air. He must have sniggered at my efforts, as a hawk must snigger when a mouse races for the shelter it won't have time to reach. I thought I could hear him give the thinnest subterranean laugh. Once more my teeth unlatched themselves and I heard my voice, babbling. Words were sputtering out of me, ones I didn't even choose.

"Tin, I'm sorry, I didn't mean it, I'm sorry Tin, I am—I fell, I couldn't help it, I didn't mean it, I'm frightened, Tin, I'm sorry—I won't tell—I won't tell!—I want to go home, Tin please, let me go home, I want to go home, I want to go home!— Tin, Tin, please, don't touch me, Tin, I'm sorry, please, Tin leave me, please, don't touch me, help me, Tin, I'm sorry, I'm afraid—"

And he did touch me: I felt his claws grip my ankle. I yanked free and howled, galloping blindly on my fists and knees, knowing I would kill him if it came to that, understanding he would certainly kill me. Stones and clods rained on my back and my head was pounding, my eyes were pouring, my throat was closing on undrinkable air. Behind me I heard him scurrying, surefooted, bounding with unhurried skill and ease. He wasn't laughing but loping in silence, no longer playing any game. It was he who decided the moment and brought things to an end: I felt his touch and whirled to face him, prepared to have it over and done.

But I whirled and whirled, the air punching out of me, squealing with surprise. Rough silver grass whipped around me and my eyes were seared by the blazing red of the sun. Over I rolled and over, my arms and legs flinging about and dumbstruck with confusion before coming finally to a sliding stop, spat from the tunnels like something gone foul.

I climbed unsteadily to my feet and stared. I could see the crest I had tumbled down but I couldn't see the tunnel's exit hole. The grass wove over it so cunningly that I hadn't even seen it from inside. Perhaps I had crawled past dozens just the same. I sank to the ground and stayed there, filling my lungs with gratitude and warming in the sun. I noted that I was covered in blood but knew it wasn't blood of my own, and the knowledge linked into the chain of pawprints with a placid certainty.

Tin wasn't anywhere. In the tunnels I had not doubted he was behind me, my toes a whisker from his razor fingers, but now, sagging in the peaceful evening and, but for the birds and fluttering insects, absolutely alone, I didn't know what to believe. It didn't seem possible that he could have been so petrifyingly there, and suddenly not anywhere. I brought round my ankle and stared at it, searching for a mark from his hand. My foot was grubby and smeared with blood and if Tin's grip had left a mark, it wasn't anything I could see.

The sun was setting and I guessed it was about six o'clock. It seemed like I had been in the tunnels forever, but it mustn't have been very long. There were a couple of hours of daylight left to me, to make a start for home. I didn't recognize where I was and I couldn't see anything built by people, but it was comfort enough that this world was my own. I got to my feet and began to walk. A buckle on my sandals had broken and the shoe flopped from my heel. I coughed raucously, hacking up dirt from inside me. Flies gathered in a cloud, entranced by the stench of me. I hummed a little song to myself and waved a flimsy hand to drive the bugs away and staggered along through the grass, resigned to walking forever and not minding if I had to, too tired to object to a thing.

But soon I found myself deep in scrub and then, pushing through it, standing on the edge of the road. I smiled amiably at it, as though it were my oldest friend, and sat down to rest awhile. I sat in a dreary, thoughtless daze, watching the ants rush about in hysteria. When I lifted my gaze and saw Da striding toward me, the sight was a curious yet sensible one, as things in a dream are skewed yet understandable. Seeing him made me want to chuckle, not because of happiness but because everything felt so charmingly peculiar. He seemed to be older and smaller than he should have been, an elderly elf of himself. "Harper," he scowled. "I told you to go home."

I nodded, wearing an imbecile's grin. "I know, Da," I answered. "And I tried to go home. I really tried."

And I told him how I'd fallen through a trapdoor and found myself in the mad black knotting of tunnels and how I had fallen out, rather than found my way out, and how I would like to go home now, if that was where he was going, and that I regretfully seemed to have ruined my new sandals.

While I told him the story I watched his eyes get bigger and bigger. When I stood up and he saw all the dried blood on me, I thought his eyeballs were going to rocket from their holes and go tearing down the road. I gurgled with laughter, remembering the pop-eyed pigs. Da looked hard at me. Then he swung away, and marched up and down for a time. I put my chin in my palms and felt myself drifting.

"Harper? Harper!"

I came awake in a hurry. "Yes, Da?"

He was still pacing, his fingers tight around the rifle and glaring at the ground. He said, "If Tin was chasing through the tunnel after you, he wasn't trying to hurt you. He was trying to guide you out to safety. That's what I reckon he was doing—and see, here you are, safe with me. Don't go thinking that other way again, hear me, chicken? Don't breathe a word of that wrong thinking ever, not to your Mam or sister or anyone. As for the rest of it, you had better come with me."

Those words he said, and what we did next— it's important to remember that Tin was Da's pet, though long gone from him and sometimes overthrown, and that the rest concerned Vandery Cable, whom Da wasn't cringing from anymore. Da

hoisted me on his shoulders and I fell asleep
drooped upon his head; I woke up as he lowered
me and found we had returned to the hog farmer's,
where Da got a shovel and handed me a spade.

From where I'm sitting I cannot see the water but if I go into the other room and kneel on the padding of the window seat I can see it glinting between the laced branches of the cypress trees, a long flat line of reflective blackish blue. From down on the sand the ocean looks, I think, exactly as I had imagined it must do, for it could never look otherwise—and yet I remember how it took my breath away to see it for the first time, how I pressed next to Audrey, meek and shyly, how I felt, at the sight of that never-ending greatness of water, somehow drowned to see it all.

Now, though, I go down to the shore every day and I'm familiar with the rock pools and the crevices, I wade into the breaking waves to the depth of my knees. Now the ocean is a companion of mine and I like to look at it, admiring how vast it is, how restless and churny. I wouldn't need to wander if I wanted to see the world, because the ocean is everywhere and touches everything, and could do my traveling for me. The water that licks my toes will be, next day, far away, lapping the coast of some exotic foreign land. But I am not a roamer, and I never have been—even at home, I never used to ramble far. I'm a bit like a stone, content to stay where it is put. Whatever was in Tin and made him such a gypsy, that thing has never been in me.

I am twenty-one years old now and for being so I was given a gold locket, which I wear on a chain around my neck. Clipped face-to-face inside the locket are pictures of my Mam and Da but every time I break the clasp to stare inside I think, instead, of my younger brother Tin. Not my youngest brother, Tin, because I always count in Caffy.

This is a strange and different place from where I used to live. Here, the strew from the cypress trees makes the earth light and feathery and it crumbles and smells sweet in your hand. Here there is often rain and thunder and the sky is thick and tumultuous for days and weeks on end. It's only after I came here, where everything is windy and waterlogged, that my heart stopped beating so furiously at my ribs and at night I would lie limp and depleted, weak with relief that I no longer endured its efforts to tear loose and abandon me. My heart is calm now, although it is an uneasy, fitful calm, like the sleep of an ailing person. Here we are far from where we once were, and years and years have gone by. I will never feel truly safe, I think, but after years I have grown tired of staying afraid. Now I am simply watching, and waiting to see what will happen.

It's only now, years later, with the fear being blunted and some space opened up in my head, that I find myself thinking, sometimes, of the pig farmer Vandery Cable. My stomach doesn't quiver now, at the thinking of his name — instead I feel a drifting ashy sorrow which is soft around its edges. It is sad, I think, that a man might have no one to mourn for him, no one to care that he is gone.

I don't want to think about this, but almost every day I do.

Da and I did a good job with the spade and the shovel that night. My eyes were wide awake after my nap across Da's shoulders but I remember my mind was moving dense and sluggish, Da had to tell me carefully what it was I had to do. Between the pendulum swings of the hogs' bulky carcasses, we caved in and backfilled the tunnel that led up to the hanging room before nailing shut the trapdoor and scattering clumps of sawdust everywhere. There was nothing suspicious to notice, once we had finished in that room. I filled a bucket with water and we washed away the blood from the cobbles, purging the stains with the heels of our shoes. In a kitchen drawer we found candles and with them we walked quickly from one end of the house to the other, pausing in each of the rooms. I held Da's hand and said nothing, too tired to ask what we were looking for. I went to take a penny I found on a bureau but he told me to leave it alone. We shut the front door when we left and you would have sworn, on seeing things, that Cable was expected to return any moment: you wouldn't have seen a clue to what had really happened to him. You wouldn't have guessed that Tin had ever been near.

We set off in thickening darkness and as we walked, my mind turned on Tin, upon the long white teeth he bared warningly, upon his strength and rending claws. I remembered the pickax Da had given him years earlier, its brutal weight, its rust and curve. Bursting from the floor beneath Cable, Tin must have seemed like a lunging tiger. You can't shake a cat that wants a piece of you and Tin would have swarmed over the farmer, the scuffle sending the carcasses slamming, Cable screaming uselessly for the station hand he'd sent away. I saw again the blood splashed on the hanging-room walls, the snubbed gristled point of the pickax. My body jerked as if I felt the strike, and Da glanced down at me. "Harper?"

Tin would have wrenched the farmer through the trapdoor without difficulty, Cable being a small man, Tin being able and strong. I clutched Da's hand tensely, struggling to keep my balance. "I'm all right, Da," I mumbled. My eyes felt round and huge as the moon, my body felt scooped hollow— I wasn't stepping on the road but floating giddily above it. In my mind I saw Cable kicking feeble as a kitten as he was towed into the tunnel and I understood, then, that if Tin had wanted to catch and harm me in the labyrinth, he could have done that easily. If he had put a hand around my ankle I would not have pulled free of his grip unless he had decided to let me.

After a time I stopped floating—after a time my legs were turned to lead. Da picked me up and carried me and I slept in his arms, sleeping through the night and the miles. Before we reached home he woke me and we washed ourselves in the creek. I took off my dress and scrubbed out much of the bloodstains and then hung it over a branch to dry. We sat side by side as we waited, the sun rising around me in my bloomers, Da plinking stones into the creek occasionally. After a long while of saying nothing, he asked, "How are you feeling, chicken?"

"I'm better now, Da."

"Good. Good . . . I've been wondering what we should tell your Mam. We don't want to worry her."

I smiled and nodded, closing my eyes to the balming breeze.

Mam was sitting at the table wan-faced and wringing a kerchief when we pushed open the door; the sight of us made her jump from her chair and a yelp of gladness sprang from her throat. She held her arms out and I ran to her, hurled myself at her, burying my nose in her hair. "He was gone," I heard Da say. "When I got to the property, the coward was already gone."

Into Mam's ear I murmured, "He wouldn't listen to me."

She stroked my head and hushed me. Later I heard that Audrey had pleaded with her to keep everything a secret, which was why none of the neighbors had come to help me stop Da on his march toward Vandery Cable's. I brooded on this for weeks, prodding resentfully at recollections in my head. I remembered the miles I had stumbled through in Da's shadow, the heat and the insects and the scratches from the trees; I recalled crouching helpless within sight of the homestead, searching for words that might persuade Da, and the fear and panic that flooded me when he banged his fist on the door. I saw again the pigs, the flecked cobblestones, the frozen moments of the tumbling trapdoor. I remembered the dark and I remembered Caffy and I remembered, most forcefully, feeling certain I was going to die. All these visions I knew I would not forget, just because Audrey wanted things—mysterious things, that no one would explain to me — to be kept forever a secret. Whatever had happened to her, I reasoned, couldn't have been so very dreadful; she could eat and talk and help with the chores and once the bruise on her cheek had faded she looked the same as always. But I myself felt bruised all over and every particle within me ached as though it had become a painful thing, just keeping my body alive.

Audrey wanted things kept secret but Cable was missing and she had surely been one of the last to see him; even if they didn't care for him, in time people at least started to wonder where the farmer had gone. He had left the hogs and house and jinker and there was a hanging room full of pork that was waiting to be salted. The more that people spoke of it, the odder and more suspicious these things began to seem. "Court," Mam said finally, sitting poised and still in her chair, "tell us, again, what happened out there. Tell us, again, what you saw."

From my place lying on the floor before the fire, I did not need to look up to know Da's eyes had darted to me. "It was Tin, Mam," I said listlessly.

"Ah!" Da exclaimed, and his hand slapped the table.

"What do you mean, it was Tin?"

"Harper, enough!"

I crooked my neck to peer at him. "We have to tell, Da. People are asking."

Da pressed his lips into thin pale lines but he knew as well as I did what needed to be done. We told the story again and this time told it true, while Mam and Audrey sat stupefied. I said almost nothing about being in the tunnels, except that I found them tangled and grim; I tried to sound as if my time down there hadn't troubled me too much at all. But we told about the trapdoor and the blood thrown all around;

we told about the deserted house and the flat cool ghostly quiet. "He did it for you, Audrey," Da finished, watching her intently. "He's always heard everything, that boy. If walls have ears, he is those ears. I reckon he heard you crying and telling your story, and I reckon he took off for Cable's in a rage. He's nippy enough to have been there and gone again while Harper and I were still walking. His instincts told him to do it, I believe—his heart, not his head. He's never harmed anyone before and I don't reckon he's likely to do so again, at least not without good reason."

"You've no proof," muttered Mam. Her hands were shading off her face and her voice was vexed with grief. "You've no proof that this happened like you say."

"Thora, that's true. There's no proof. But if you had been there, as were Harper and I, I don't reckon you could believe anything else. Isn't that right, Harper?"

I chewed my lip and said nothing, watching a slater scramble frantically the length of a smoking log. The heat on my face was making my eyes water and I saw swimming reflections of everything.

"There being no proof will be good for us," said Da, mutedly. "It will be good for everyone."

Audrey, in her corner chair, had been silently weeping. Now she smeared a wrist over her eyes, crushing flat all the tears but for a stray that shivered from her chin. She said, "We have to save Tin. I want him to be safe. Da, I'll say whatever you think I should say."

He and she turned to Mam but I stayed watching the slater. It shuffled about and reared at the flames, its creased shell streaked with color. I wondered if Mam was thinking of how she had lost Tin such a long time ago, how he had never afterward needed a mother. He did not seem to care for her, nor for the sadness he'd caused. She must have loved him anyway, and believed him still her child. I knew without looking that she agreed with Audrey because when she nodded she caused a ripple in the shadows around the room. The slater rolled off the log and landed in a cushion of ash.

From then on we had our story, and stuck unswervingly with it. Cable had been bedeviling Audrey, Audrey had come home. Da had gone to argue it out and discovered Cable flitted. This was almost the truth—it was hard to put a finger, exactly, on where the falseness lay—and Audrey, I think, soon stopped bothering to remember how things had actually been. Soon I could not mention

Tin's link to the tale without her frowning at me with no understanding, cocking her head blankly. In her mind, the untrue story became the way things had been, herself an innocent, Da the heroic, Mr. Cable so craven. I don't reckon she remembers at all, now, that evening when the slater ran the log.

So we told the story and the story spread, touching down like a locust plague wherever it found the opportunity. The authorities came and heard it and went away again, puzzled but empty-handed. To me the tale sounded so full of holes that I longed to laugh scornfully at anyone who believed it. I began to see that people, like cattle, can be led by the nose. And then one day, when months had passed and almost no one mentioned Cable, Jock Murphy was lolling on the veranda relaxed as a sunstruck cat when he said, "You know what everyone's saying, Court?"

Da stiffened, and reached for his flask. "No, I don't, Jock. Tell us."

"Everyone's saying that wherever Cable ran to, he's still running. They're saying that, when he heard you were coming to exchange a few words, he took off faster than his jinker could move, that's why he left it behind. He recollected he was only a hog man, you see, and that you yourself are a soldier. He could prance in lecturing you about this and that, but he couldn't teach you a thing about looking after you and yours. You've become the most admired man around here, Court. Everyone's in awe of your honor, coming to your lass's defense like you did."

"Is that what they're saying?" Da puffed himself out.

"Certainly it is. And that's what I'm telling them happened, as well. When I hear someone talk about it differently, I'm quick to put them straight."

Da gazed at Murphy. He said, "I never laid a finger on Cable, Jock."

Murphy smiled shrewdly. "Righto, Court. I believe you."

My heart was battering choppily and I wandered off, bouncing a rubber ball and pretending to be composed, but beyond sight of the house I ran berserkly helter-skelter, hot air gushing down my throat and grass lashing my stumbling knees. We would never be set free, I reckoned; we would be haunted, eternally.

Autumn flagged and winter sulked after it and despite the eggs the chickens laid and the milk we got from the cow, we found ourselves sometimes cold and vaguely hungry. I didn't complain, though, not like I used to. Some things were, to me, less important than they had been; I was thin, and twitchy as a dying fly, but being cold and hungry no longer had power to plague me. I worried, however, that Mam and Da and Audrey did not feel the same, and when Devon sent a letter but apologetically no money I exhumed the notes I had buried nearly a year previous and been saving for emergencies, and gave them to Mam. Audrey cut short her glorious hair as well as her old dresses, trimming them all over until they fit onto me.

It was a cool spring evening the last time we saw Tin. I had not searched or called for him since the moment I'd rolled out of the tunnels. I knew I should not be afraid of him and I believed he had no wish to hurt me, but I could never think of him without a tremor. I could never quite smother an image of him lunging, of his raised striking arm, or stop hearing the whistle that traced the arc of the pick head as it rent the air.

The nights came early on those tender spring days and we were tucked into the house by evening. To give myself other things to think of I had returned to writing my stories and Audrey would read them page by finished page, correcting my spelling with a red-inked fountain pen. This particular night I was writing and Audrey was improving, Mam was darning and Da was tacking a patch of leather to the sole of his shoe: these ordinary things we were doing when the dogs let loose a booming, each of us settled in our private meditations and in no way expecting what was next going to happen.

Mam got up to open the door and I glanced without interest over my shoulder, reckoning on seeing a tramp or one of the neighbors. Instead, a small scuffed creature was lit by the lamplight slanting from the door and the dogs were milling around him, sniffing his feet and wagging their tails. The creature held a great bundle of something tied up in a rag. For a moment we stared, not recognizing him, but who else could it have been, is what I wonder now, who else but wandering Tin. We saw his naked limbs, his waxy skin, his discolored hair, his hooking razor-sharp nails. He raised lashy eyes to us and we saw the lined face of an old man, a face on its way to another world. Da murmured, "Jesus."

It was Tin, who was mythical, and he looked just that way. He looked nothing like the boy he was supposed to be, ten going on eleven. He seemed to hover above the earth somehow, the curious glow of his flesh illuminating him. I would not have been surprised if wings had opened up behind him and he'd shown that he could fly.

Whatever it was he cradled in his arms he placed carefully on the veranda and stepped backward, holding his eyes upon the thing as if wary of it getting away. After a moment, when he seemed surer it was safe, he looked into the room at us. He looked first at Mam, then Da, then at Audrey, then me. When his eyes settled on mine I felt something inside me shake free, and go to him. I didn't give it—he wanted it, and it went to him. Then he smiled, only slightly, but enough so we agreed, afterward, that we had seen it done. With that he turned and vanished and the dogs barked but didn't go.

Mam bent, and peeled the wrapping from the bundle. Audrey and I stood at her elbows and Da brought over the lamp. In the flickering light I thought I saw the wrapping move and I guessed what the bundle was then, a baby. Tin had filched a baby thinking Mam might fancy to keep it, having lost so many of her own. The idea left me reeling with both glee and dismay.

But, the rags off, we found nothing except a lump of dark earth. I was relieved and disappointed about the baby. Da leaned down and prodded the clump with his finger. "What is it, Da?" I asked.

He didn't reply. He hefted the earth and the burden of it made him stoop. It hadn't made Tin stoop, he had held it easily as a little animal, but Da swayed and winced his way across the room before dumping the load in the washing water. "Oh, Court," Mam scolded, because the water had been dirty and was now splashed out everywhere, but Da paid no attention. He grabbed the cloth and began sponging the dirt. Audrey held the lamp up and we all gathered around.

And the four of us were bent over the basin with the lamp pouring its yellow light onto our heads, each of us bursting to ask questions but not saying anything so the silence of the room was, in an instant, almost unbearable, when a piece of earth sluiced away from the lump and the glitter of gold broke through. I remember the glint was a lively, living thing, a dragonfly that flashed around the room, a sprite winging its way on the lamp beam and returning to settle brightly on the crest of its brilliant home. Inside the hunk of dirt lay a gnarled, besmirched, pitted, and boot-sized chunk of gold.

I gripped the rim of the basin, teetering on my heels. Mam clapped her apron to her mouth and the lamp slung down to Audrey's side. Da stepped clear and we gazed at it, that mighty and spectacular nugget rising from its lake of filthy water. The moment was only that, a moment—for Da whooped then, catching Mam in his arms and making her dance crazily around the room, his bare feet thumping the boards—but it is the moment I wish could have stayed forever, when we stood staring at our fortunate future and none of us were talking or even breathing, turned to stone by the incredibility that was Tin's gift to us.

And then when Mam and Da were dancing and Audrey had her head thrown back and was laughing, a black bird of ingratitude darted through me, swooping out of nowhere and flashing away just as sharply, chattering with a voice that has not spoken to me since. It cried that it was cheated, that this was a coward's way of concluding the story. I think that voice belonged to the child I was, and she did not come with me when I left the land. I think she is still out there somewhere, rebellious in her rage, scouring the tunnels for Tin.

Everyone decided that was what Tin had been doing all those years, prospecting. They reckoned that the catacomb of tunnels, the life lived so lonely, those big flat watchful eyes, all these things and everything else were purely devoted to gold. That's cods, of course. The nugget was something Tin found in his travels; having no use for it, he had no reason to keep it from us. He must have known that his gift would change things, and maybe make us leave him. He must have decided that he didn't care, if such a thing was to happen. He already had what it was he wanted; he was already content. Tin dug, and I've always believed it, because digging was what he was born to do.

Not all things happened, though, the way he might have expected them to.

The four of us talked all night about the life awaiting us within the nugget. While Da composed a letter to summon Devon home, Audrey said her deepest wish was that we could go away. I said I would like that, too. "Oh Mam," I said, clinging to her and hopping on my toes excitedly, "let's go somewhere far away."

Mam nodded, understanding. "But where? Where would we go?"

"We should go to where the ocean is," I decided dreamily. "We would have a little house and live on the edge of the sea."

And that's what we did, that's why I can see the ocean from the window, that's why Audrey and I are here. It's only she and me, just the two of us. I didn't honestly believe it would happen, but Mam made sure we got away. I write to her often, urging her to come here, but she says she should not leave Da. He needs someone to look after him, she explains. He'll tire of digging eventually, she says, and then both of them will come and things will be better that way, she won't have to worry. Da, you see, has been bitten by the mining bug, and spends his time scratching feveredly at the land. He thinks there must be plenty more, wherever the nugget came from. Tin's gold was a fine thing, but it wasn't enough to content our Da.

It has been a long time since I've seen either of them, Mam or Da. It has been years. If not for the tiny brown pictures that I've closed inside my locket, I would have forgotten the look of their faces.

The ocean is dazzling, as I knew it would be; the

first time I saw it, it dazzled me more than my first sight of the gold. I sit on the sand and watch the waves roll and I think about everything that happened to my family and me. The mudslide, the shanty, the cows, and poor Caffy, each so different and spread far apart, but also so tightly entwined. Each fits into the other with the simple neatness of a pin. Looking back, life seems, in its way, like a fall from a great height, the outcome decided even before the event is begun. I love to be here, where I feel finally secure, but often my heart jolts and wrenches, tripping on its own memories.

I miss the muzzy faces of our dogs. I miss our house, the way it shone in the sun. I miss my Mam and Da. I miss Devon, who has gone to the front, and I miss Izzy, my sister's elusive sweetheart, who is also fighting the war. I miss that little girl, too, the small one who stayed behind.

And I miss Tin, who would be a young man now but is, in my memory, still a boy. Devon writes that they could use someone with his gifts at the frontline, someone who could scoop the trenches smartly. Devon is joking: we are all glad Tin is safely underground, plowing past the bones of cavemen and dragons, a young boy only because I haven't seen him for years. But sometimes, just

lately when I've been sitting quietly and remembering everything I had to know, I think I have felt the
slightest waver and heard, so softly, the shifting of
the sand. The soil here is grainy and loose and the
ocean makes a roaring sound which must travel as a
murmur for miles underground. I have put my
hands to the earth to feel for him; I have put my
ear to the ground to listen. If Tin steps one day
from the earth, dusty, blinking his pale clear eyes, I
will be the first thing he will see. His hand will be
dirty when he places it in mine, and mine will not
be clean.

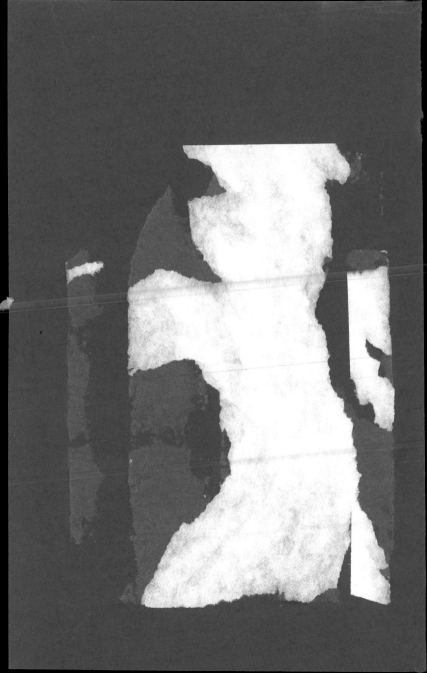